I0712482

EACH PIECE OF

FIREWOOD

EACH PIECE OF

FIREWOOD

KIAN SABIK

Also by Kian Sabik

The Huntdown Duology:

Endangered

Abandoned

Each Piece of Firewood
Copyright © December 2023 by Kian Sabik

All rights reserved. Printed in the United States of America. No part of this book may be used or reproduced in any manner whatsoever without written permission except in the case of brief quotations embodied in critical articles or reviews.

This book is a work of historical fiction. Apart from well-known real people, events and places, all names, places and incidents in the narrative are products of the author's imagination or are used fictionally. Any resemblance to current events or living people is entirely coincidental.

Content warning: there are mentions of torture, death and violence. Please take caution.

Cover Design: Ebook Launch
Map Credit: Eshal Mughal

ISBNs:
979-8-9866864-6-2 (Ebook)
979-8-9866864-7-9 (Paperback)

First Edition: 2023

10 9 8 7 6 5 4 3 2 1

GLOSSARY

Assalam Alaikum: Muslim greeting that means "peace be upon you"

Alhumdulillah: Muslim saying that means "Thanks to God"

Dhuhr: One of the five Muslim prayer times

Jumu'ah: The Muslim prayer on Friday afternoon

Sayar: Burmese for "teacher"

Tatmadaw: The official name of the Burmese army

Walaikum Salam: Response to Assalam Alaikum

N
W
E
S
NGLADESH
Dhaka
MYANMAR
Maungdaw
Naypyidaw
Rakhine
State
Bay of Bengal
THAILAND
INDONESIA
Bangkok
Tarek's Journey, 2017

PART I:

BEFORE

CHAPTER 1

TAREK

HOPE IS A snake, wrapping itself around your heart, squeezing. Every day, its hold gets stronger and stronger.

Until finally, you have to tell yourself to let it go.

But after it unwraps itself, it leaves you empty, hollow.

It leaves you...dead.

I swallow the rock in my throat and scratch my tongue against my teeth, trying to rub the sandy bumps off. I stare at my book, my fingers turning white from gripping onto my pencil.

Tick.

Tock.

Tick.

Tock.

I watch the minutes tick by; the pencil tapping against the table. The eerie bubble around my ears bursts, the familiar sounds of giggling and clattering dishes luring me back into reality.

I turn around, watching as Grandpa tickles Haya. A smile tugs at the corner of my mouth. Grandpa's eyes meet mine.

"Tarek?"

"Yes?"

He smiles at me, the gap between his teeth sucking the light from his grin. I shudder, remembering the soldier's fist landing on Grandpa's mouth, the tooth flying out.

"Take a break. You've been sitting here for more than two hours. Move around, enjoy the sunset."

My limbs loosen at the thought of relaxation. I nod.

I pick up my books and set them inside the cabinet next to me, stretching my tight back.

Knock. Knock. Creak.

My brother pokes his face into the room. He nods to our sister, grandpa and then to me.

"Dinner time," he mutters before ducking behind the door.

"Alright, my little girl," Grandpa lifts Haya off the ground by her feet. Her hair touches the floor, and she strains her neck to look up.

"Stop!" she shrieks, the smile growing wider on her face. She brushes her hands against the floor.

I turn the doorknob and the smell of food crashes into my nose. My stomach shrieks.

Haya dashes forward and grips my leg. "Up." She lifts her arms.

I smile and heft her up until her eyes reach mine. She pokes my nose and giggles. I throw her up, her delightful screams piercing my ears.

"Again. Again."

"It's dinnertime, silly." I place her on my shoulder and walk through the hallway until I reach the kitchen. Mama puts the last plate on the cloth on the floor. Strands of black hair stick to her forehead and she drops, leaning against a wall with her eyes closed.

Ali sits down next to her. Beside him, Grandma grunts as she sits in a chair, a toothless smile spreading across her face.

I place Haya next to Grandpa, taking a seat next to her. I reach for Grandma and Haya's plates, the fish gently flopping onto them.

For the next few minutes, the sound of spoons clanging against the plates echoes throughout the room.

Eeeee.

I drop my spoon down, cupping my hands over my ears. Haya scratches her spoon against the plate, unfazed by the sharp noise.

"Here, let me help you," I say as I reach for her spoon. I scoop some fish into it, holding it in front of her mouth.

She zips her lips tightly, turning her face. "I'm a big girl. I can do it myself," she pouts.

I glance toward Mama and she nods. "Don't make a mess."

Haya's face lights up, the pout instantly disappearing. Mama smiles tiredly, her eyes stuck on Haya. A sigh escapes her lips. She catches me staring at her and her eyes dart toward her plate.

But she can't hide it from me. She can't hide the pain, the grief. I can see it in her eyes. It's been there ever since Papa died when I was seven.

That was ten years ago.

CHAPTER 2

KAN

YOU STARE OUT the window. The sun sinks out from the horizon, its deep red calling to you. It's just like your dreams.

You reach out, watching your fingers line up on top of the sun. It's as if you can touch it. It's as if you can touch your dreams. They're so close.

A week. Just a week and then you'll finally be free. You'll finally be able to join the Tatmadaw.

Your mother wouldn't let you become a soldier until you turn eighteen. She wanted you to get a proper education, just in case you couldn't reach your dreams.

You've been counting the years since that conversation.

"Kan?" Mama calls from downstairs.

"Yes?"

"Can you go out for groceries please? We don't have enough fish."

You trudge down the stairs into the kitchen. Mama crouches down, peering into a cabinet. She grunts as she lifts a pot onto the stove and smiles when she sees you.

There's a certain glow in her eyes. You've never understood that subtle, calming radiance before. As if she knows that the future holds peace, just like the past few years.

'Going away will devastate her,' a deep voice tells you, but you ignore it.

Mama swipes a strand of hair off her face and hands you some money. "Here."

You bob your head slightly and step out the front door. Streaks of orange and pink run through the sky, the fresh air rushing into your legs.

You sigh, making your way to the market.

CHAPTER 3

TAREK

BEEP. BEEP.

I reach out from under my blanket to turn off my alarm clock, rolling out of bed. I cover my mouth as a deep yawn radiates from me. I tiptoe toward the window, sticking my head into the curtains.

I watch the streaks of red paint the brown and green landscape, my mind slowly waking up.

Click.

I slide open the window, inhaling the raw air. I stand there for a few moments, gazing at the world around me. The world that seeks to eliminate us.

The approaching sound of stones rolling under small wheels resonates in the air. I peer to the side, catching a glimpse of the newspaper boy. He reaches into a basket, throwing a white roll in front of our house.

Thump.

I tiptoe out the door, watching Ali's chest rise and fall rhythmically.

Creak.

The door slides open and I reach for the newspaper. I glare at the headline.

ALIENS INVADING OUR LAND!!

Since the late 1900s, the Rohingya have been plotting to take over Myanmar. These people are Muslim and extremist, believing in violence and terror over peace and security. Since the Myanmar State has been formed, the Rohingya, whom we have generously allowed to live in Myanmar, conspire to overthrow the Burmese government and establish their own violent regime. Our lives are under threat. The Rohingya claim that they advocate for peace, like us Buddhists, but we have all known those are lies to blind us from the truth. Buddhism advocates for peace but allows us to defend ourselves from those who want to hurt us. We need to rid ourselves of these varmints and clean our country from their evil. We should advocate for their exile, especially after the Arakan Rohingya Salvation Army, or ARSA, has risen and spread chaos throughout the Rakhine State. This group proves that the Rohingya don't deserve all the Burmese have offered them. We beg the Burmese government to listen to our cries of protest and if they don't, we will take matters into our own hands.

Thump.

Thump.

Thump.

My heart pounds in my ears. I crumple the paper in my hand. My ears start to burn.

Sccrrr. Scccrr.

The paper rips apart in my hands, the little pieces of white floating to the ground. I rest my forehead against the wall and inhale.

Tick. Tock. Tick. Tock.

The clock in the kitchen resonates throughout the house. I sigh, pick up the shreds of paper and throw them in the trash.

．　　　　．　　　　．

I reach into the fridge for the carton of eggs with the headline burned into my mind.

Aliens?

The comic books from my childhood come to mind. People have always been searching for aliens, searching for ways to communicate with them. Humans want to *befriend* aliens. At least, that's how the comic books depicted it.

But when we are called aliens, it's a bad thing. People don't want us. They want us to disappear.

And extremists? How are we extremists? If these people had actually studied world religions, they would understand that Islam is a religion of peace. We don't side with ARSA or any other terrorist group.

My heart boils with anger as I crack the egg on the pan, the white spreading across the surface. The oil sputters, its screams echoing throughout the kitchen.

Creeaak.

Creeaak.

I glance over my shoulder to find Haya tiptoeing toward me. She hugs my leg, peering into my eyes. I smile at her and bend down.

"Aren't you supposed to be sleeping?" I ask.

"I don't want to," she whispers, shaking her head. She moves her long, dark hair away from her face.

I stand back up and take my egg out of the pan. "What do you want to eat?" I ask her.

"What you're eating."

I take a step but lose my balance. "You have to let me go if you want breakfast," I laugh.

She squeezes harder. "No."

I moonwalk to the fridge and crack another egg. I fill two glasses with milk, holding one out to her. She glances up at me.

I smile at her. "If you want to drink it, you have to let me go."

She peers up at me with her shining blue eyes, her hands unclasping from my leg. Haya hops to the floor cloth, sipping the milk.

My eyes shift toward Haya. She looks like a normal Rohingya girl, except for her blue eyes. Our great-grandmother's eyes.

I smile softly, my eyes trailing down the cracks behind the stove. They're like rivers, winding through a forest. A forest of words that leads to a sea of knowledge.

The crackling coming from beside me floats me out of my thoughts.

"No, no, no."

I toss the black egg onto a plate and facepalm. Something grabs my shirt from the left. I open my eyes to see Haya barely peeking over the counter. Her smile fades away as she glares at the stiff, black breakfast.

"Here." I hand her my unburnt egg. "That one is mine."

Her radiant smile returns, and so does the twinkle in her eye. She gallops back to the cloth. A slight smile spreads across my face.

A few moments later, I sit on the floor, trying to keep a straight face as the blackened egg turns into ashes in my mouth.

"Tarek?" Haya peeps.

"Hm?"

"Is that yummy?"

I gulp. "All food is yummy."

Haya examines my face for a second. "Can I have some fruit now?"

I nod, and she skips to the small fridge under the sink. A red apple appears in her hand and she bites into it.

"Mmm," she says.

I slap my hand over my mouth, trying to stifle my laughter. I peer over my shoulder, locking eyes with Haya. She stares at me, her head cocked slightly to the side.

"What's funny?" she asks.

I turn back and gulp air, trying to force the laughter out of my stomach. "Nothing, nothing. You looked funny while you were eating."

I blink as silence engulfs the room. I glance behind me to see Haya standing a few feet away, her shoulders slumped and her eyes watering.

The smile from my face disappears and I walk up to her.

"Do I really look funny?" she whispers, her eyes glittering.

"No, no. Of course not," I crouch down to meet her eyes, "You're the most beautiful girl I have ever seen." I wrap my arms around Haya and she sinks into me.

A few moments later, I let go. The sadness still hangs in her eyes and it stabs my heart.

"I'm sorry," I say.

She nods and walks out of the kitchen. I lift myself off my knees and wash the dishes, the image of Haya's wet eyes still glued to my mind.

CHAPTER 4

KAN

PEOPLE BOB THEIR heads when they meet your eyes. It's as if they can see your power, your authority,

Your future.

Your smile creeps toward the corners of your eyes with each passerby.

Until you see her.

You glare at the little girl. You cringe at her brown skin, at the loose hijab on her head. Her disheveled hair and her smile. Her sharp laughter as she plays with her friends.

You see red. You see your hands around her throat. Her struggling in your arms.

You warp back into reality, still glaring at the girl. She notices you and smiles. That makes the fire in your heart spread.

You shove your hands into your pockets, forcing yourself to continue moving. Mama needs the ingredients for dinner today.

But you can't help thinking about that Rohingya girl. She deserves to die. She deserves to have her blood run down the street.

You clench your hands into tight fists as you approach the store. Inside, you throw fish, apples and anything else you see into the basket.

You step toward the cashier and hand him the grocery, your mouth still pulled into a scowl.

"Everything alright?" he asks, his forehead crinkled with concern.

"Mind your own business," you mumble.

The cashier freezes for a split second and then cautiously continues. He analyzes you, throwing the grocery into bags. He hands you the bags. "Have a great day, sir," he mumbles.

You grumble in response.

You step out of the store, into the darkening sky.

.   .   .

Creeeeak.

You turn the knob and enter your house.

"Kan? Is that you?" Mama calls from the kitchen.

"Yes," you reply.

She steps toward the entrance. Her face lights up when she sees the bags in your hands. You hand them to her.

"Thank you, my son." Mama embraces you. The anger in your heart melts away as you sink into your mother's hug.

You nod.

She searches deep into your eyes. "What did I do to deserve such a good child?"

I chuckle and kiss her forehead. "Let's make dinner."

CHAPTER 5

TAREK

KNOCK. KNOCK.

I look over my shoulder. A tall, muscular man leans against the wall, his arms crossed across his chest. A full dark beard spreads from his chin and his dark eyes glare into my soul. A deep scar runs across his hand, reaching up into his arm. I can still picture the knife slashing his skin, a river of blood flowing down.

"Someone is up early, as usual," Uncle Yusuf booms.

I smile at him and nod, turning back to the sink.

Uncle sits down on the floor. "Why do you wake up before sunrise? No one is awake at this time."

I put the dishes on the rack and dry my hands with a towel. "I don't really know. It's just so much more peaceful in the morning. Everything is fresh and new. You get to experience things you don't see normally, like the sunrise and the warm breeze."

"You're just like your father," he says, with a hint of pain woven in his voice. I stand near the sink, my feet pointing toward the door.

"I won't keep you. Go on with your day," Uncle grunts and makes his way toward the stove.

I bob my head and step out of the kitchen. Streaks of sunlight poke through the window, tickling my face. I crack open the cabinet and out comes a stack of old books.

My father's books.

The books he spent countless hours reading and taking notes on, hoping to spread knowledge to the world.

The books that are the only part of his soul down on Earth.

I run my hand along the crisp pages, as if expecting for time to warp backward. As if expecting for Papa to come back.

I open my eyes, disappointed that I'm still in the living room. Disappointed that I'm not back in the past.

Scccrrrr.

Aunt Harsa sits down near me, her hands hanging on top of her knees. "Assalam Alaikum, Tarek," she greets.

"Walaikum Salam," I respond.

"Is everything alright? You're pale."

"Of course. Everything is fine."

I try to smile, but I can even feel how fake it is. She analyzes me for a few seconds before getting up and going into the kitchen. I take a deep breath and lock eyes with my math textbook.

CHAPTER 6

KAN

YOU DROP INTO your seat, the steaming pot in front of you calling out. You glance toward Mama, noticing her eyes cast toward the table.

"You're almost eighteen," she murmurs, her eyes still locked on the wood surface.

You nod, your mouth suddenly dry.

"Do you still want to enlist in the Tatmadaw?" she asks.

"Yes," you whisper.

Her voice is hushed. "Are you sure?"

You nod. "I've always been sure."

She turns her head up toward you, her heavy, somber eyes peering into yours. "But I'll be all alone," she whispers.

A rock scratches down your throat.

"And what will I do if you...you're killed?"

You put your spoon down, the clank echoing in the hollow room. You lock eyes with your mother, her eyes filled with shock.

"Mama, I'm going to die sometime, anyway. At least I'll die serving my country."

Mama's mouth drops slightly and she freezes. After a few seconds, she smiles and nods. "I'll always be right here. You can always come back to me."

Her smile doesn't reach the corner of her eye.

CHAPTER 7

TAREK

I LEAN MY head against the wall. My brain begs for a break.

I glance toward the clock. *9:36 a.m.* It's too early. There are still a few hours until noon.

My stomach says otherwise. It growls and yawns. I walk into the kitchen and grab some milk. I pour the white liquid into a stained glass, hefting myself onto the counter. I drain the liquid. My stomach stops gurgling.

The sound of faint giggles comes from the other side of the house. Light, quick footsteps echo through the hall and a voice calls out. "I'm going outside," Haya announces.

"Be back for lunch," Grandma replies.

Creeaaak. Thud.

The door shuts closed. A gust of warm air flies into the house, carrying the scent of coriander, chilies and lemongrass.

The smell of the village.

Even when I'm accompanying Grandpa to the neighboring towns, I can always smell when we're close to home. That's the beauty of a home. It's the heart's true north, always pointing toward its direction. You always know you have a place to go back to.

You know you can always go back home when it's too much, when you need to savor the warmth of family.

Beep. Beep. Beep.

I cup my hands over my ears and press hard. The sharp beeping screams throughout the house. I jump down from the counter and search the hallway. I turn the corner to find Mama violently punching her phone's screen.

The screeching stops. I cautiously take my hands off, the sound still ringing in my ears. Everyone else floods into the living room.

"Sorry," Mama apologizes, "I set the wrong time for my alarm."

"Why is it so loud? Everyone will wake up," Grandma asks.

Mama draws with her foot on the floor. "I'll fix it right now."

Grandma nods and goes back to her room. Mama clicks on her phone, absorbed into the screen. My heart still pounds as I go back to the living room.

.   .   .

The pages of my book flip, slamming shut with the cover. I lift myself off the floor, stretching my tight back and shoulders.

Creeaaak.

Light footsteps scurry toward me and tiny arms grip my legs. "Tarek?" Haya says.

I look down. "Yes?"

"There's a woman being mean outside," she whispers.

I shoot straight up and in one giant step, I'm out in the sunlight. My eyes set on a Burmese woman shooting daggers at the children playing in the street. Her eyes are cracked red and her fingers are curled into a fist. She lurches out and grabs one of the children.

"Help! Help!" he shrieks but everyone turns away. Some of the children run toward him, tugging on his shirt.

I step toward the woman. She glares up at me.

"Please let go of the child, ma'am," I say, trying to keep my anger suppressed.

"And who do you think you are?"

"I'm an older brother who's trying to protect these children."

"What power do you have over me? This child attacked me."

I shake my head. "No, he didn't. *You* attacked *him.*"

"And how would you know that?"

"I saw you."

She clenches his teeth. "Who will believe a dark *Rohingya* boy over me, a respected Burmese woman?"

I curl my hand into a fist, trying to release the fury. I inhale sharply. "Please let go of this child or else I will have to call my uncle."

"So what? He can kill me? Is that what you want? Do you want to see my blood flowing down this street so you can drink it?" she spits.

The woman releases the boy. "You Rohingya are monsters. These children will grow up to be violent, feral creatures. You'll be drinking our blood one day. I know you're waiting for the perfect moment. They should do away with you all. One day, the government will come for you all! Do you hear me?" she screams as she retreats into an alley.

Thump. Thump.

I gulp air, trying to soothe my racing heart. I crouch on one knee, my eyes reaching the little boy's. "Are you alright?"

He nods furiously. I smile and pat his shoulder. "You were very brave."

His eyes sparkle as he grins.

A hand pulls at my legs. I glance down to see Haya peering into my eyes. She grins like a little monkey. "I'm hungry."

"Let's go make lunch, monkey," I respond. I reach down to get her arms off my legs.

Her nails dig into my bones. "I'm not a monkey." She pouts.

I clench my jaw to keep from yelping. "Yes, you are."

Her nails sink deeper into my flesh. "I'm not."

I grab her ankles and pull her up, her head pointed toward my feet. "You are my little monkey and you always will be," I laugh.

She reaches for my leg, but I shake her. She screams, a grin spreading across her face. I haul her up on my shoulders and make my way to the kitchen.

I grab a pan. "Can you grab the bread for me, please?" I ask Haya.

She hops to the fridge and throws the bread at me. It lands on my face, a snort escaping from my nose. Haya blinks and breaks down, giggling. I close my eyes and laugh too, a blanket of joy wrapping around the house.

CHAPTER 8

KAN

YOU EXHALE AS you enter your room.

You've kept it bare ever since you've known you're not going to stay here.

Outside, blue streaks run through the murky, reddish sky. A few sparkling dots wink at you and the moon lifts itself into the sky. The sun yawns, laying down. The sound of dishes rattling against each other downstairs reaches your ears.

You collapse onto your cot, savoring every sensation in your house. In a few days, you'll be eighteen. Your dreams will finally come true. So why does it feel so bad? Why are you doubting yourself?

You shove those thoughts out of your restless mind, but it resists. You have to keep sight of your goals. You've been dreaming about this since you were little. You can't give up now. You can't give up when you're this close.

You close your eyes, trying to go to sleep, but it runs away from you. You sit up. Mama always told you to walk around or do something relaxing until you're sleepy.

You tiptoe out of your room and into the kitchen. On the dining table, you spot today's newspaper. You were so busy you forgot to read it. You pick it up, flipping through the pages until a headline catches your eye.

ALIENS INVADING OUR LAND!!

Your eyes swallow the words until you reach the last letter. You put the paper down, your hand resting on your chin.

You can imagine the outburst caused by the article. Everyone would be enraged, but for different reasons. The Rohingya would think this is a lie. The pure Burmese would feel that the Rohingya deserve to leave.

But no matter who thinks what, the hatred in your heart overtakes all else. The Rohingya are criminals at the end of the day and criminals don't deserve to live here.

You place your head down on the table. You should go back to bed. You're finally sleepy.

CHAPTER 9

TAREK

KNOCK. KNOCK.

I crack open the door to see Grandpa and Ali's soft eyes looking back at me.

"Assalam Alaikum," I say and swing the door wide open.

"Walaikum Salam," they respond and slip their shoes off.

We walk to the kitchen, sitting down with everyone else. I catch Haya trying to get my attention from the corner of my eye. I glance toward her, holding my laughter as I catch sight of her goofy face. She holds it for a few seconds before breaking into giggles.

Grandpa talks about his day at work and how much Ali has improved at fishing.

"Tarek will come with me and be my assistant when Ali opens his own shop," Grandpa says, smiling toward me.

I shake my head and swallow a bite of the vegetable stew. "I want to go to university. I want to learn and be a teacher," I say.

Grandpa, Ali and Mama stop eating and glance toward me. The uncertainty in their eyes stabs me. I nudge Haya. She brightens up. "Can I be in your class?" she asks, leaning forward.

I smile and nod. "Yay!" she screams.

Mama flashes a half-smile at her but her concerned face returns. Grandpa clears his throat. "Tarek?" he says.

"Hm?"

"You know we don't have the money to send you to university, right?" he mumbles.

"I know," I say.

"How can you go to college without money?" Mama asks.

"I'll get a scholarship. I'm willing to work too. Whatever it takes."

"But what about the fact that very, very few Rohingya are admitted to universities? What if you aren't accepted?" Ali asks.

"I'll see then. Right now, I'm aiming to be among those few." I turn toward Mama. "Mama, you know how much Papa cared about us getting a proper education. He wanted us to be successful. He wanted to see us break past the market and go farther in life."

I gulp hard. "You know how badly he wanted to be a teacher," I whisper.

Silence.

Complete, deathly silence.

I squeeze my eyes and glance up.

Grandpa and Mama look at each other, the look that parents exchange when their children talk about unicorns and princesses. The look that means that their children will understand when they're older.

My heart squirms inside my chest.

"Okay," Grandpa says and the rest of dinner is spent in silence.

.   .   .

Grandpa grunts. "Time to go back to work. Let's go, Ali."

As soon as the door locks behind them, everyone is left in silence. Mama helps Grandma to her room. Haya smiles at me. "I'm going back outside," she announces.

I nod. "Are you going to come?" she asks.

"After cleaning up."

She skips out of the house, leaving me alone on the floor. I lift myself off the floor, picking up all the dishes. I wash them in silence, wondering what the future holds.

.   .   .

I turn the handle on the sink, the water abruptly stopping. I rub my hands against the towel and walk out of the kitchen. From the other side of the house, I hear hushed voices. I step toward the front door and rest my head against the wood.

"I'm worried about him. He dreams too big. He doesn't know how reality works yet. He thinks he can go to the moon, but he doesn't see how that's impossible. Saleh was just like him: unrealistic. And look how he turned out. He was forced to become a fishmonger, just like Pa, Yusuf and Ali. The Burmese will *never, ever* let a Rohingya man advance. They won't see how bright and hardworking Tarek is. All they will see is his race. That's it. They've never let a Rohingya climb the ladder of success before, why would they give that opportunity to Tarek?" Mama says.

"Let him. You never know if he will succeed. Maybe he will be the first person from here to go to the moon." Grandma chuckles.

"Ma, this is a serious matter. His whole future will be ruined if he continues like this. He doesn't have any practical skills. He doesn't know how to sew, how to fish, or how to farm. All he knows is that his books are in the cabinet over there. That won't help him in this world."

"Maybe those books will be the key to him advancing. We've always been a family of fishmongers. Maybe he will be the first to go to university and advance in the world."

Just as I'm about to step out the front door, a sharp, bloodcurdling scream pierces the air.

Aaaaaaahh.

CHAPTER 10

KAN

YOU WAKE UP on the table, your head pounding. You glance toward the clock.

4:56 a.m.

You force your eyes open.

Discipline is key to becoming a soldier. Waking up at 5 a.m., no matter how much you slept that night. Being able to endure any physical, mental and emotional obstacle. Being able to think fast. Not backing down in the face of challenge.

You jump in place, trying to get the sleepiness out of your system. After a few minutes, you shake your limbs and grab breakfast. A single apple.

They don't give you much food in the military so you've been practicing. An apple for breakfast, some bread for lunch and fish for dinner. If you get hungry at any other time, you eat some nuts. This is the way of the warrior, the soldier who serves his country.

You splash cold water onto your face and crack open the door, pausing for a second. You listen as Mama gently murmurs in her sleep.

You smile slightly and step into the sunrise, your footsteps fading away.

.   .   .

The air in your lungs burns, scratching against your throat. You slow down, giving your legs the smallest bit of relief.

Almost there. Almost there. You tell yourself but you know you still have a mile left. You stop for three seconds, catch a few breaths and continue through the town.

.   .   .

Click.

You slide your key into the door and it slides open. You peek inside, listening for your mother's gentle snores but her door is open. You step inside the house, locking the door behind you.

"Mama?" You call out.

Silence.

Your heart pounds as every possible situation runs through your head.

Someone could have broken in.

She could be sleepwalking.

She could be in the bathroom.

Maybe she went to get water.

You tiptoe toward the kitchen, sticking your head inside. A smell travels to your nose.

Flash.

The ceiling lights explode on.

"Surprise." A voice laughs from near the stove.

You rub your eyes.

"I made you breakfast," Mama exclaims.

"But...I already ate," you respond.

"You can eat again. You're going to leave in a few days. Don't you want to eat your mother's food? Who knows what they're going to give you in the army."

You force a smile, burying your grimace deep into your stomach.

"Come on. Let's go eat," she says.

Her grin warms your heart.

CHAPTER 11

TAREK

I THROW OPEN the door and the screams get louder. I jump into the street to find Haya hollering, crystal tears streaming down her cheek. I wrap my arms around her tightly, muffling her screams into my shirt.

"Shh, shh. It's okay." I pat her back as she slowly calms down.

Haya breaks free from me. "They took her. They took Salma," she cries. Her eyes water again.

"Who took her?" I ask.

"The people with the guns."

My blood grows cold and my tongue becomes stiff. I force myself to open my mouth.

"Where did they ta—"

Another scream breaks out, this time more pained than Haya's.

"Don't move," I tell Haya and run toward the scream. Each louder note plays right before my eyes, the *thud* of my footsteps echoing with the *thump* of my heart. Blurs of brown and black *whoosh* past until I reach the climax of the agonizing shrieks.

An alley.

The screams are now laborious, duller. The wet, heavy, sewer-like stench from inside slaps my nose and I grip my stomach, holding back my vomit. Gentle, minuscule scurrying inches toward my ear and the silhouette of a tail emerges from the light.

I jerk back.

A whimper comes from the end of the alley. I barely make out three shadows. A small ball-like object is on the ground and it shuffles. Two towering figures bury their heels into its stomach and it groans in pain.

Click.

Everything flashes white as a flashlight comes to life. The faces of two men come to light. In their eyes, there's a red hunger accompanied by a bloodthirsty smile. One wears clear glasses while the other is short and stocky. Both rest their hands on their pistols.

Near their feet, there's a young girl, about four years old. Tracks of pink streak down her face and her lips are cracked. She stares at me, despair heavy in her eyes.

"I would turn around if I were you," one of the soldiers warns.

My feet refuse to move, sinking deeper into the dirt. Soon, it's as if my entire body is stuck in the mud, every single muscle refusing to cooperate.

"You wouldn't want something to happen to you, would you? *Turn around now.*"

I gulp and glance down toward Haya's friend. Her eyes beg me, glistening in the white light. I rip my eyes off her and stare at the two soldiers.

My heart hammers against my chest. The two soldiers glare at me with their devilish eyes, as if they can see my helplessness and desperation.

As if they can see my sheer, unfiltered terror.

"Salma!" a voice calls out from the alley's opening. My eyes widen and I jerk backward to find Haya standing there. The air from my lungs rushes out. The edges of my vision blur. I glance back at the soldiers. They stare at Haya, their grins widening.

"No!" I scream and dart toward Haya.

Click.

The sound from behind me propels me forward.

Whoosh.

The soldier's arm raises upward.

Crack.

The thunder crash ripples through the air, deafening me. A small object zips right past my ear, lodging into the house in front of me.

I tumble to the ground, my arms grabbing for Haya. I roll in the dirt and run but not before glancing back.

For a split second, the flashlight turns toward Salma, lighting her widened, shocked eyes.

Click.

The light turns off.

CHAPTER 12

KAN

"DID YOU PACK everything?" Mama asks from her room.

From the end of the hall, you can hear the floorboards *creak* and gentle footsteps arrive at your room.

"You've packed your clothes, toiletries, towels, a pillow, some food, your phone, passport, important documents, and money?"

You nod as she continues down the list. You know you haven't forgotten anything. You've been waiting for this moment for years.

"If you forget anything, text me and I'll mail it to you," she says.

"I have money, Mama. I'll buy something if I need it."

You can see the heaviness in her eyes. "Don't forget to call me when you can," she whispers.

You give her a hug, your chin resting on the top of her head. But you don't say anything. You don't want to make a promise you won't fulfill.

She sighs. "Okay. I'll drop you off at the train station tomorrow morning. Get a good night's sleep, okay?"

You nod even though you know you won't be able to sleep. You're too excited to sleep.

Mama closes the door behind her and you lay down on your cot, your imagination going wild.

CHAPTER 13

TAREK

"NO. NO. NO. *No!*" Haya screams at the top of her lungs, her voice deafening. She digs her nails into my arms, still screaming.

A sharp pain emerges from my shoulder. "Ow," I yelp but hold on tighter. I tilt my head slightly to see Haya's jaw clasped to my shoulder. Tears stream down her red face and angry grunts come from her.

From the surrounding houses, eyes stare out from the windows. I bite my tongue as Haya continues biting down, trying my best to get back home as fast as possible.

I throw open the door to find four pairs of shocked eyes staring back at me. Mama, Aunt, Uncle and Grandma stare at Haya, then me and back to Haya. Mama grabs her from the arms but she screams louder.

"Let. Me. Go!" she shrieks and slaps Mama's hands away. I look up to Mama in horror but she steps back quietly. Grandma, Aunt and Uncle try but Haya pushes them back.

I beg them with my eyes and for a split second, everything is quiet.

Until a flash of pain shoots up my arm.

"Ow," I shriek and drop Haya. She shoots between my legs and lurches toward the door. I grip her arm and tug her back toward me, gripping both of her arms in one hand and her legs in the other.

She kicks, punches, screams, bites but I hold her tighter and tighter. I struggle toward the kitchen and release her. Haya takes the chance and tries to run out but I grab her again. I gently place her against the ground, pinning her down as her face lights on fire.

"Enough, enough," I whisper into her ear but she continues as if she didn't hear me.

"Enough," I say louder but she continues shrieking.

"Enough!" I yell.

Silence.

Complete silence.

Haya stares at me, her face pale. I let go of her and wrap her in a hug.

"I'm sorry," she whispers.

"No, I'm sorry. I shouldn't have yelled," I respond, "I know you're upset. I know you've lost someone you loved, but I had to get you out of there. I can't let them take you too."

"You left her," she mutters.

I suck the tears back inside. "I know. I had to. I had no choice."

Life is a game, a match of chess. You lose pieces, you eliminate players, you make sacrifices. That's how life is here. The Burmese seek to kill every Rohingya in their path because they're different.

"I'm tired," Haya says, resting her head against me.

"I know."

I rub her back until her gentle snores break through the silence. I carry her to Mama's room and lay her on the mat, pulling the blanket up to her shoulders.

I reach out to pull the curtains over the window, peeking outside at the bright world. The sun is a red ball, hiding behind some houses. The leaves rustle in the breeze. Such a perfect day but the black clouds have to come and rain sadness down here.

I pull the curtains tight and step out of the room, but not before glancing back at Haya.

CHAPTER 14

KAN

BEEP. BEEP.

As soon as your alarm rings, you shoot out of bed. The excitement in you courses through your veins. You've never been this jittery since the parade when you were nine.

Downstairs, you can hear Mama whispering on the phone. You tiptoe to the bathroom, getting ready. You brush your teeth for four minutes, making sure they're extra clean. You brush your hair and shave.

You examine yourself in the mirror. You've grown so much. You've turned into someone unrecognizable. As you stare in the mirror, you hear Mama calling for you.

"Kan. Kan. Hurry up. You have to eat."

Click. Creak.

You close the bathroom door behind you and gallop down the hallway. You enter the kitchen, where you see Mama waiting on the dinner table. On your spot, there's a plate of eggs, toast, meat and milk. Your mouth waters but your discipline takes control.

They're not going to give you real breakfast in the Tatmadaw. You need to continue with your habit of barely eating.

"Please, my son. Eat. I know you think this is too much, but this is the last time I'll cook for my child," Mama begs. Her voice cracks.

You nod and watch as a sad smile spreads on her face. Anything to make your mother and country happy. That is where your loyalty and obedience lie. That is your goal in life.

That is why you were born.

You sit down and savor your mother's food for the last time.

CHAPTER 15

TAREK

AS I CLOSE the door behind me, six figures wait by the door. I look up into everyone's anxious faces.

Tap. Tap.

Ali taps his foot against the concrete floor, biting his lip. "What happened?" he asks.

Everyone else nods.

"Let's go sit in the living room first. We don't want to wake Haya up," Grandpa suggests.

I sigh and follow everyone there.

.   .   .

Grandpa reclines on the chair as he sighs, rubbing the bridge of his nose. "Tarek, I know this is scarring, I know it hurts." He nods at me with gentle eyes. "I know you think this is your fault...but it's not. It's not your fault."

I swallow the boulder in my throat, my whole body light as if it's suspended in the air.

The horror on Salma's face when she realized that I wouldn't...couldn't help. The hopelessness, the defeat in her eyes.

"Can I go to sleep now? It's late," I peep.

"Of course." Mama gives me a quick hug. "Don't bother about waking up early tomorrow. Take your time."

I nod and head to me and Ali's bedroom. I lay down on my mat, keeping my blanket near my feet. I hug myself and close my eyes but every time I do, Salma's bruised face, her whimpers and her tearful eyes haunt me.

I push the sight away and try to relax into the mat, waiting for day to dawn.

.   .   .

"Tarek. Tarek. *Tarek.*" A figure rattles me. "Wake up."

My eyes flutter open and I groan.

"Hurry up. It's ten o'clock," Uncle says.

"*Ten o'clock,*" I yell and roll off my mat. I throw on a pair of clothes and gallop to the kitchen. My head pounds.

You've slept way too much. You should have stayed awake when you woke up at six.

I beat myself internally as I make breakfast. "Someone finally woke up late today for the first time," Uncle sings. I smile, trying to suppress the regret boiling in my stomach.

Aunt calls Uncle from the living room and he walks out, leaving me alone with my thoughts.

I eat in silence, stuffing the food Mama left into my mouth. I glare at the clock as each minute ticks by.

10:06.

10:07.

10:08.

10:09.

"Tarek?" Mama calls from her room.

I place my plate in the sink and stick my head into her room. "Yes?"

"Do you mind doing the grocery today? Yusuf just left to join Grandpa and Ali."

I nod. "Here's the money." Mama hands me a few coins and bills.

"I'll leave right now," I say.

"Can I come too?" Haya asks from behind me. I turn to look into her cracked, red eyes. I glance toward Mama and she nods.

"Let's go." I hand Haya her shoes and we exit the house.

CHAPTER 16

KAN

THE TREES FLY by like blurs, and the wind pushes against the car, the *whoosh* ringing in your ears. Mama focuses on the road and you gaze at the scene around you.

It's the last time you'll be able to see it in a long time.

You glance to the side at Mama every so few minutes, catching a glimpse of tears flooding in her eyes. You don't have the courage to tell her anything because you're happy.

You're happy to move forward in life.

It's a dream come true. But...you have to sacrifice something. You don't have the heart to tell her you'll sacrifice your own mother for your dreams.

.   .   .

After half an hour, Mama pulls into the train station. You take your seatbelt off, but Mama doesn't move.

"This is your stop," she whispers, the sadness heavy in her eyes.

You nod.

"This might be the last time I see you."

You nod again.

"Are you sure you want to go?" she asks.

You nod.

"Are you absolutely sure?"

You give her a hug. "Yes, Mama. I'm absolutely sure. I'm not a child anymore. I know what I want to do."

You try to let go, but her grip grows tighter. You want to get to the stop as fast as possible. But Mama doesn't let go, even when you try.

"Mama?"

"Hm?" she says quietly.

"I have to go now. I don't want to be late on my first day."

"I don't want you to go. Who'll take care of you?"

You sigh. "Mama, I'm not little anymore. I can take care of myself. You have to let me grow up. I can't be a child forever. I can't be with you forever."

You cover your mouth as the words rush out. Mama's heavy, shocked eyes, lock onto her knotted hands on her lap. You were too harsh.

"Okay," she peeps.

"I didn't mean it," you whisper.

"You did," she responds, the hurt in her eyes spreading.

Beep. Beep.

The cars behind you shriek angrily. Mama nods. "Goodbye, Kan. I hope you don't let your independence and ambitions get to your head."

You pull her into one last quick embrace. "Take care of yourself."

You try to walk slowly to the building, but the anticipation drives you forward. You glance back one more time, expecting to see the familiar black car.

But the spot is empty.

Mama's gone and your life has started.

CHAPTER 17

TAREK

THE SUN IS bright yellow outside, scorching everything it touches. I squint in the light, Haya's hand in mine. I glance down toward her, analyzing her frown and empty eyes.

"Hm." I try to get her attention. She looks up with a puzzled expression. I heft her by the arms and place her on my shoulders.

"Hold on."

She squeals and even though I can't see her, I can sense her smile.

"Look, Tarek. I'm so big," she exclaims.

"Yep. You're even bigger than me," I laugh. "Since you can see everything, you have to tell which way to go."

After fifteen minutes, we arrive at the market. I buy fish, vegetables, fruit, milk, eggs, everything we eat on a daily basis.

"Tarek?" Haya asks, her voice thin. She's going to ask for something.

"Hm?"

"Can we get some *pira*?" she asks slowly.

"Do you see it?" I ask.

"Hm."

"Okay." I lift her off my shoulders and onto the ground. "Lead the way, captain."

She lights up and marches deep into the market. I follow her tiny footsteps until she stops in front of a stall.

Haya points at the coconut cookies and turns to me, begging with her eyes. I rub the bills in my pocket. Barely enough for one cookie.

I nod at Haya. "One *pira* please," I ask the seller. He hands the cookie to Haya, and I hold out the money. Haya's eyes brighten and she gobbles the cookie in one bite. The seller blinks rapidly, wide-eyed and then bursts out laughing.

"Here," he hands Haya another one, "I can see you really like *pira.*" He smiles toward me. "Don't bother about paying."

Haya glares at it.

"What are you supposed to say?" I nudge her.

"Thank you," she exclaims, and the seller grins.

"Of course, my daughter."

I bob my head toward the *pira* seller. "Thank you, sir."

He smiles back at me and then moves on to the next customer.

"Let's go." I turn toward home with Haya's hand. She repeatedly ventures in the opposite direction, getting distracted by the chickens, fish, fruit, anything interesting. I have to tug her back on track until finally, our wood home is visible on the horizon.

.   .   .

"We're home," Haya announces when I open the door.

Grandma comes out of her room and gestures for me to give her the bags.

I smile, taken back to when she and Grandpa were younger. When they used to play games with us, when they laughed with us. That was until three years ago, when their age caught up to them. The only excitement in their lives now is seeing what we got for grocery and dinner time.

"Haya. Come take a shower," Mama says from Grandma's room.

"Can I play outside first?" Haya whines.

"It's late. You don't have time to play outside *and* take a shower today." Mama comes out of the room. "Come on."

Haya drags herself to the bathroom with Mama. I place the grocery in their proper places. The fruit, eggs, milk, and fish go into the fridge, the flour goes into the cabinet and the bags go into the trash.

As I throw the plastic bags away, a letter lies on the counter catches my eye. I crack open the seal and devour the words.

To whom this may concern,

You have received this letter because you identify as a Rohingya. As you know, every six months, we require you to update your household list. Take a picture and number everyone present in your household, whether they're family or not. In the list, include their names, age, occupation and relationship to the owner of the house. We will be verifying the list and doing checks on each village. If we find any evidence of evasion or false information, they will be exiled and may face the threat of execution.

This is due by the end of the week. A carrier will arrive at your village at the end of the week to pick these up and the following day, soldiers will do their rounds.

My heart stops. Even though it's been years since they've been doing this, it still sends chills down my spine.

I force my feet off the ground and walk to Grandma's room with a heavy heart. I hand her the letter.

She doesn't even have to read it to know. She nods, her anxious eyes imprinted in my mind.

CHAPTER 18

KAN

AS SOON AS the doors swing open, the bustling ring of people, machines and announcements hit your ears. You inhale the sharp, industrial air, your heart jumping with excitement.

"Excuse me?" you ask the first worker you find, "Where's the check-in desk?"

He points down the hall. "Go through there and it should be the first thing you see on the left."

You bob your head. "Thank you."

You glance down at your watch. About half an hour before the train is set to arrive. You walk up to the check-in desk with your phone in hand, your excitement barely contained.

CHAPTER 19

TAREK

AS SOON AS Mama steps out of the steamy bathroom with Haya, she freezes when her eyes lock with ours.

"What's wrong?" she asks, articulating each and every letter.

Grandma hands her the letter and Mama's eyes move left and right as she scans it. Her arms fall to her side and she leans her head back, closing her eyes for a split second.

"Okay, let's get this done as quickly as possible. Ma, can you please get everyone to the living room? Tarek, grab the numbers from my closet. They'll be on the bottom next to the suitcase."

I nod, my footsteps echoing against the mud floor. I throw open the closet and crouch on the ground, rummaging through the corner near the decades-old suitcase.

My hands brush against the cardboard rectangles. I tug and they fall out.

"Tarek, are you coming?" Grandma calls from the living room.

I stand back up, dragging myself into the living room, where everyone's waiting. Mama's tapping her foot against the dirt, deep in thought. Uncle bites his lips while Grandpa picks at the skin around his nails.

Grandma swats his hand. "You'll damage your skin."

Grandpa's hands swing by his side as he relaxes them.

Mama grabs the stack from me, handing each person their appropriate sign. The lower the number, the older the person. Grandpa clips the string behind his neck, his sign painted a bright red number one.

Mama crouches down to fasten the sign around Haya's neck.

"It's itchy, Mama," she pouts.

"I know, I know. It's just for a little bit." She directs her attention to everyone else. "Alright. Get in your positions and no smiling. Let's try to get this done in one go."

I squeeze myself in between Ali and Uncle, the people in the line beside me getting shorter and shorter. Mama positions her phone on the bookstand.

"Everyone ready?" she asks.

We nod. She clicks a button and rushes toward her spot.

3.

2.

1.

Click.

The camera flashes a white light and I force myself not to blink. A millisecond later, Mama reaches for the phone, holding it up for everyone. We crowd around her.

"Up, up," Haya says, and I heft her up.

In the photo, our solemn expressions are pasted across the screen. I can see the camera flash in each person's pupils. Our stick-like arms echo from the picture, highlighting our poverty.

I gulp hard.

It's as if the Burmese can see right through us. Like they can see us completely naked in the picture.

My blood grows cold thinking about it. The humiliation of it all. I clench my jaw and try to calm myself down.

"Does it look fine?" Mama asks.

"As fine as taking a population control picture can be," I murmur.

Mama's eyes soften. "I know, my son. I know. But we can't do anything about it. We can only try to abide by the rules, hoping not to be targeted. That's all we can do."

I swallow my words and nod. I just simply nod. There's nothing else we can do. We can only accept our situation and live the best, the happiest we can.

A few moments later, Mama breaks the silence.

"I'll cook dinner," she says. She smiles at Haya. "Do you want to help me?"

Haya smiles and nods, skipping to the kitchen. Grandma retreats to her room.

"We've got to fix our cart. The wheel fell out of the axle," Grandpa announces, and Ali follows him outside.

I'm the only one left in the living room. I glance outside the window. The trees shade the sun and the sky gradually turns into a shadow. Orangish lights illuminate from people's windows, the silhouettes inside laughing and playing.

Creeeeaaaak.

I turn my head at the slowly opening front door. Aunt's head peeps into the house. I can feel the color drain from my face.

"Assalam Alaikum," she smiles.

"Tarek? Whose voice is that?" Mama asks as she steps out of her room. Her face turns pale when she locks eyes with Aunt.

"Is something wrong?" Aunt asks.

"You weren't here? You weren't in the picture?" I stutter.

CHAPTER 20

KAN

BEEP. BEEP.

"Attention. All passengers bound to Da Nyein Gone, please board train D4. Again, all passengers bound to Da Nyein Gone, please board train D4. Train D4," the woman in the announcements announces.

You grab your bag and stand on the edge, over the tracks. From the distance, a gray box zooms forward and countless windows and doors fly past you.

Whoosh.

The doors in front of you crack open and everyone clamors toward them. A knot settles in your stomach and something inside it flutters.

"Come on. Move it," a scratchy voice from behind commands.

A hand finds its way to your back and you're shoved through the door. Inside, velvety seats lay in front of you and people settle in. Families sit together, the kids staring outside with their fascinated eyes.

The wonder in their eyes softens yours. Soon, the ground beneath you starts to move and you sit in the seat next to you. You watch as the station grows farther and farther and soon, you're just as awestruck as those children.

CHAPTER 21

TAREK

"WHICH PICTURE?"

"The population control picture," I respond.

Aunt's face drains into a bleached canvas. "You didn't notice that I was missing? Can't you take another one?"

"We were swept into the chaos of it all. Yusuf is on his way back home," Mama responds.

Aunt collapses onto the floor cushion, putting her head between her hands. "What do we—what do I do?"

Mama disappears behind the kitchen wall, the clatter of objects shifting reaching my ears. "We don't have enough money to print another one. We sent the money Pa made with Yusuf..." Mama's voice trails off as she sees Aunt's panicked face. "I'm so, so sorry."

Aunt tries to smile, but the glistening in her eyes says otherwise. "I'm going to my room," she whispers and everyone lets her.

.   .   .

Tap. Tap.

I rip my eyes off my history book and crack open the door. Outside, there's a muscular man with a bag slung on one shoulder. His eyebrows are crinkled together.

"Yes?"

His eyes meet mine and it's like looking at fire. "I'm here to collect the household lists," he says in a deep, vicious voice.

I nod. "Let me wake my grandfather up."

I reach to close the door but he grips it, throwing it open. "Do you seriously think I will wait for *you?* Now, give me the list now or else I'll leave."

I nod, a boulder lodging in my throat. "Yes, sir."

I bolt to the kitchen, grab the papers, and hold them out of the door. "Here you are, sir."

The man rips them out of my hands.

"Hm," he scoffs and storms to the next house.

CHAPTER 22

KAN

"THE NEXT STOP is Da Nyein Gone. Again, the next stop will be Da Nyein Gone."

The seats beside you are silent, the families having left a long time ago. The landscape is now gray with the buildings. You sink into your seat, trying to quell the tingling in your stomach.

You shift to your side, trying to distract yourself. Outside, you gaze at the sky painted with white and gray speckles. Patches of raw green dot the land as you zoom past them.

Beep. Beep.

Your phone vibrates against your hand. You turn the screen.

Mama:

Let me know when you get there.

You swipe the notification away and turn the screen back down. You've still got a long way to go.

. . .

"Attention, passengers. The stop for Da Nyein Gone is twenty minutes away. The stop for Da Nyein Gone is twenty minutes away. Please be ready to exit the train. Thank you."

You glance down at your watch. *10:12 a.m.* You'll be there around 10:30. You stretch your legs and slouch in your seat.

Scenarios run through your head. What if you aren't accepted? What if you fail the physical examination? What if they don't need you? What will you do then? What if you have to go back home? It'll be humiliating.

You shake your throbbing head. You haven't even gotten there. Whatever happens will happen. Focus.

In the distance, you can see the glint of metal and the train starts to slow down. You reach down for your bag and stand up. As the train comes to a stop, you grip the seat in front of you. Your legs wobble and you lean forward.

And then everything stops.

The doors near you *hiss* open. You peek your head outside and step out of the bubble of warmth.

.   .   .

"Excuse me?" You ask the man in front of you. He's wearing a green cap and, on his nose, lies a thin frame of glasses. He's absorbed in a pamphlet and if he heard you, he doesn't show it.

"*Sir?*" you ask again, irritation woven into your voice.

He turns his head slightly toward you, his eyes still glued to the paper.

"Yes?" he mutters in a hoarse, deep voice.

"Where are the military headquarters?" you say. The man's cold eyes glare into yours and you stare back.

"Continue down this road and turn right at the first traffic light you see. It'll be the biggest building on the road."

You bob your head to show your appreciation, but you stifle a grimace. People are so rude these days.

He nods and turns back to his pamphlet. You speed walk down the street, your nerves propelling you forward. Your heart jumps with every step and your stomach sinks deeper and deeper.

You turn right, your eyes searching for the building. You tilt your head toward the sky-high building and your heart climbs up into your throat.

There it is. There's the culmination of years of dreaming and working.

You rub your hands together and wipe your forehead. You take a deep breath and reach forward for the handle. Behind you, your suitcase trails and your backpack drums against your back.

Here it goes.

CHAPTER 23

TAREK

I GLANCE UP at the clock every few seconds. Anxiety wraps around me like a suffocating blanket. The air around me gets heavy, refusing to enter my lungs.

Tick.
Tock.
Tick.
Tock.
Creeeak.

I let go of the breath I was holding in. Gentle footsteps echo through the hallway and Grandpa tiptoes away from the rooms. He nods toward me, focused on the kitchen.

I stand up, the mud floor beneath me growing small.

"Grandpa?"

He turns toward me with his refreshed, gentle eyes. "Hm?"

"Today is Friday, right?" I ask, hoping it sparks a memory.

"Yes?" He looks perplexed.

"Today was the day they were supposed to pick up the lists, right?"

His eyes widen.

"They picked it up while everyone was asleep," I blurt.

He nods, but doesn't say anything else. "You're not worried?" I ask.

He sighs. "There's no point in worrying about something that already happened. Besides, all you had to do was hand it to him. Did you eat already?"

I nod.

"Are you planning to do anything today?" Grandpa asks.

"I want to finish this book on Aristotle's natural theories." I pause. "Why?"

"Do you want to accompany me to work? Ali wants today off. I tried to tell him that when he's older, he's not going to have a break but he fell asleep. He does deserve a break, though. It's been months since he's had one."

Grandpa smiles at me with hopeful eyes. Something inside me squirms. I don't want him to go alone. Besides, a change in location might be good.

"When do we have to leave?"

.   .   .

"Are you ready, Tarek?" Grandpa calls out from the kitchen. I finish packing some food and throw my hat over my head.

"Yes, Grandpa."

"Alright. We'll leave in five minutes," he says.

I make my way to Mama's room to see her holding Haya. Grandma is on the bed, massaging her legs.

"I'm going with Grandpa today," I announce in the heavy silence. Mama and Grandma smile and nod. Haya looks up at me with wet eyes.

"No. You can't go," she screams. She jumps off Mama's lap and grips my legs.

I kneel down. "I'm not leaving. I'm going with Grandpa for work." I pat her back.

"No, you can't."

"I have too."

Haya digs her nails into my ankle. I yelp out in pain. "Where did you learn this from?"

She scratches deeper and clenches her teeth. "Stay with me."

Mama appears beside me. "Haya. Let go of Tarek. You're hurting him," she orders, but Haya completely ignores her.

"You can't go," she mutters with clenched teeth, tears streaming down her cheeks.

Mama grabs her from her waist. Haya thrashes in her arms. "You can't go. You can't go. You can't."

"I'll see you in the afternoon," I say and run out of the room. I glance down at my left ankle. My skin is red with four angry cuts. I shake my leg and go outside.

CHAPTER 24

KAN

CREAK.

The first thing that hits you is the smell of the polished floor. You cautiously approach the desk, absorbing every sight. The desk and floor glimmer, the light from the ceiling bouncing off them. The staff are wearing crisp suits and the latest computers are spread across every empty counter space.

"May I help you?" A woman asks.

"I'm here to sign up for the military," you say, still examining the office.

She flashes a tired smile. "Go through that door and through the first door to the left. You'll find the recruiter there," she responds.

You nod.

As soon as you enter the double doors, the atmosphere changes. Everyone is stiff, serious. The air is full of the smell of coffee and paper.

You try not to melt right there and then. You gulp hard and enter the room on your left. A man sits at the desk in a suit. His blazer is spread on his chair and his hand rests under his chin, his eyes glued to the computer screen.

"Yes?" he asks, raising his eyes over his glasses.

"I'm here to register for the army," you try not to wheeze.

"Alright. Take a seat."

The man gets up and reaches behind into a carton. He takes out a thick packet of paper and hands it to you.

"Fill this out and then"—he pauses as he glances at his screen. "Oh, I guess I have time for an interview in a few minutes. Let me know when you've completed this and I'll interview you."

You nod, the black ink marking the paper.

.   .   .

"I'm finished, sir," you say and hand him the clipboard.

He glances over the pages, speed reading everything.

"Alright. I see nothing in the form that we should go over. I think you're an excellent candidate." He stands up and sticks his hand out. "Congratulations. You've made it this far in your enlistment. Tomorrow, you'll have your physical examination. If you pass, you'll be an official soldier and your training will begin immediately."

You shake his hand, hoping he doesn't notice the thick layer of sweat. If he noticed, he didn't say anything.

"Go outside and tell the lady at the desk that you're cleared for the examination. She'll lead you to a place where you can sleep."

"Thank you, sir."

He nods and immediately goes back to his computer.

You go back through the double doors and to the desk.

"Yes?" the same lady from before asks.

"I'm ready for the examination tomorrow. Where can I sleep?" You ask, more relaxed and confident this time.

"Let me show you to your room." She searches her desk until she finds her keys. She gestures for you to follow her.

CHAPTER 25

TAREK

I PULL THE wooden cart as beads of sweat drip down my face.

"We're almost there," Grandpa remarks calmly.

Ahead of me, there's a forest and the sound of running water reaches my ears. The birds chirp while the wind rustles the leaves. The pink sky is tinted with blue and the sun is half white and half red.

Grandpa's grunt lures me out of my thoughts. His head is the only thing I can see. The rest of his body is down the steep decline.

"Tarek?" he calls out.

"I'm here," I respond.

"Give the cart to me. This part is difficult. I don't want you to slip." He holds his hands out and I give him the cart.

I grip the trees around me as I descend near the riverbed. Grandpa is soon standing next to me, putting rocks under the cart's wheels.

"I've lost a good many carts to this river," Grandpa chuckles. He grabs two fishing rods and tosses one to me.

"You know how to fish, right?" he asks.

I nod. Uncle taught me when I turned ten.

"Our goal is to catch at least thirty for the day. We have a few hours before we have to go to the market."

"Thirty fish? In a few hours?" I ask with wide eyes.

Grandpa laughs. "Yes. That's not much, actually. Watch how much fish we'll have after a while."

I nod but the amazement still rushes through my mind. I sit down on the grass, watching the forest around me come alive. On the trees, squirrels scurry on the branches. The birds flutter near the water and the occasional deer jumps through the trees.

"You haven't come out here for a long time. I can't even remember the last time you came with me," Grandpa remarks.

I chuckle embarrassed. "I'm focusing on studying right now."

Grandpa nods but doesn't say anything. I know he thinks my studies are pointless, but he hasn't stopped me from pursuing university...yet.

Grandpa's rod swings in the opposite direction and he hauls in a massive fish. He tosses it into the cart. At the same time, something tugs at my rod. I place my fish into the cart too, replacing the bait on my rod.

"You said you wanted to be a teacher, right?" Grandpa asks, breaking the silence.

I nod. "What do you want to teach?"

"I want to teach little kids. Kids a few years older than Haya."

"You're good with kids," Grandpa remarks, "I think you'll be a great teacher."

"Grandpa?" I ask.

"Yes?"

"Can I ask you a question?"

"Of course, my son."

My throat goes dry. "Why...why don't you want me to go to university?"

I peer to my side, watching Grandpa stare intensely at the water, as if expecting the fish to spring out toward him.

"Tarek, you—I do want you to go to college." He still doesn't meet my eye.

"Then why were you quiet during dinner when I said that?"

His response comes out in a low murmur. "After you see what I see, you begin to doubt in hope." He meets my eyes. "After you see the horror and cruelty lurking in people's hearts, you start to doubt that there's any compassion left."

Grandpa pauses for a few seconds. "I know you're a smart, capable young man, Tarek. I can see the hope radiating from your eyes. But I'm afraid that once you go out into the real world and see what it's like, once you see others rejecting you again and again and again, your hope will fade into the darkness. And then, you'll be like me, a hopeless old man who's waiting for death. I don't want you to be like that. I don't want you to face that horror. I want to protect you, just like your father would if he was here."

I swallow hard. A lone, crystal tear drips down Grandpa's cheek. We sit on the riverbed, in complete silence, the gentle chirps of birds fluttering in the air.

CHAPTER 26

KAN

THE WOMAN CLOSES the door behind you, leaving you in the room. It's no bigger than a closet with a cot on the floor. On the wall, there's a piece of paper.

You walk up to read the words written on it.

If you need to use the restroom, it's at the end of the hallway on your left.

You collapse onto the cot, not bothering to unpack your stuff. The tingling in your stomach has disappeared, replaced by exhaustion. You stare at the ceiling with your loose limbs refusing to budge.

2:14 p.m.

You've still got hours before you have to sleep. Might as well explore the city.

.   .   .

You arrive back to your room at eight. You were hoping they provided dinner but just in case, you bought some *shan* noodles.

You sit down on your cot, stuffing the food into your shrieking stomach. Your phone lights up with a message. You wipe your fingers with a napkin and tap the screen.

Mama:

Is everything alright?

You wipe the other hand and type rapidly.

Me:

Yes. Got here safely. Have my physical exam tomorrow.

Mama:

Let me know how it goes. I love you <3

Me:

Love you too.

You shut your phone down and close your eyes, the world slowly turning dark.

.   .   .

Knock. Knock.

The tapping on the door jerks you out of your sleep. You wipe your sweaty face and run your fingers through your hair.

You crack open the door, making sure the person on the other side can't see you. "Yes?"

The woman from yesterday appears. "A bus will take you to the facility. It'll be here in half an hour."

You nod, your tongue thick and bubbly. You grab your backpack and head to the bathroom.

Inside, you violently brush your teeth and scrub your face with ice-cold water. You brush your hair, moving it to the side, leaping out of the bathroom. Within a few minutes, you have your suitcase and are waiting in the lobby.

The earlier you arrive at a place, the better. You hate being late and even getting there on time is not good enough for you. You need to be there at least ten minutes early. You never know what can happen and it's always best to be prepared for everything.

You sit down on a chair, waiting for the bus. The anticipation eats at you as you watch each second pass by on your watch.

After twenty grueling minutes, a blue bus hisses in front of the entrance. You jump up, grabbing your things and stretching as the bus' doors swing open.

Finally, it's here. And two minutes early.

You glance over your shoulder. Outside, the humid air bites at your skin. The driver nods and smiles at you, a few passengers scattered near the windows.

"Moment of truth," you whisper as you enter the bus.

CHAPTER 27

TAREK

JUST AS GRANDPA said, we caught thirty fish. Actually, we caught forty-five. I stare in awe at the cart, a huge grin spread on Grandpa's face.

"Let's go to the market now," he says and grabs the end of the cart. "I'll handle the cart until we're back on the road. I don't want you to get hurt."

Grandpa grunts quietly as he hauls the cart up the incline. As soon as the ground levels up, he lets go and exhales deeply. I grab the cart and follow him down the scorching road.

The sun is now close to its peak and the brightness of everything stings my eyes. My hands burn but I continue pulling the thousand-pound cart behind me.

"Everything alright?" Grandpa asks, a patient smile on his face.

"Yes," I respond, trying to hide my sweat.

"Would you like help?" he asks, knowing that I do.

"No, thank you. I've got it."

"Are you sure?"

I smile. "Grandpa, I'm here to help *you*, not the other way around."

He chuckles but lingers closer. I try to speed up but the heat holds me down.

What I would do to be at home, reading about philosophy, history, science, literally anything. The trees around me turn into a blur as I focus on my thoughts, picturing Aristotle's theory about the Earth being the center of the universe.

After a grueling twenty minutes, we reach the shade of our stall. Grandpa sets up the cart and places two chairs in front of it. Everyone is setting up their shops, barely a person or two roaming around. Next to us is the tailor with bright colored cloth hung around his shop. On the other side, there's the fruit seller, the aroma of the freshly picked fruit lingering in our space.

Grandpa gestures toward the chair next to him. "Take a seat. It'll be a while before we get a rush here."

I sit down, taking in the scene. The market is so different through the eyes of a seller. It's not the open expanse of shops but now, a small, shaded area.

Grandpa gets up as an elderly woman hobbles over here.

"Assalam Alaikum, Fatima. How are you?"

"Alhumdulillah, my son. How are you?" she responds, her voice raspy.

"Alhumdulillah. Here's your fish." Grandpa hands her the biggest fish in his cart.

The woman nods, smiles and goes back the way she came.

Grandpa turns toward me. "She was an old teacher of mine back when they had schools for the Rohingya. Her husband died a few years ago and since then, she hasn't been able to make much money. She comes here every morning to get fish."

Both of us sit down again, waiting for time to pass. After an hour, a wave of people floods into the market. Along with them, a few Burmese soldiers wander around, their rifles stiff on their shoulders.

I watch as some kids make their way to a candy shop. A Burmese man peers over his stall. He shoos them away, a fire burning in his eyes. He catches me staring and shoots daggers at me.

I quickly turn away and after a few seconds, glance back at him to make sure he still isn't looking. I shift my eyes to the fruit seller next to us. A teenage girl, no older than me, approaches him, her eyes searching the fruit. He glares at her and furrows his eyebrows.

"How dare you touch my produce?" he yells, and she jerks back.

The fruit seller grabs the apples she touched and throws them at her. "Don't come here again. Do you hear me?"

The Burman fruit seller grumbles angrily to himself and I stare at him dumbfounded.

Grandpa catches me staring, wide-eyed, but doesn't say anything. A few more customers stop by our shop, half of the fish now gone.

The Burmese soldiers laugh as they make their rounds. They walk up to the *pira* seller and take a basket full of *pira,* not paying for a single one. The man looks upset for a split second but then focuses on the next customer.

"Please," a whimper comes out from among the crowd.

The bustle of the market evaporates, leaving us in complete silence. Grandpa freezes, his hand frozen in midair.

"Please," the female voice pleads. All eyes toward her and the soldier gripping her hijab.

But no one dares to move.

The soldier's fingers tighten on the scarf and he tugs, ripping it off her head. The young woman screams in pain, my blood turning cold.

People begin to go in the opposite direction,

But I can't move. My eyes refuse to turn away, fixed on the dull orange cloth and the clump of hair hanging from the soldier's hand.

CHAPTER 28

KAN

"ATTENTION," A MUSCULAR, tall man in green shouts on a raised platform. The buzzing around you instantly grows quiet, all the young eyes facing the man.

"You all are here because you stand with your country. You, young, bright men, are here because you support your country against all its enemies. You left your families, your homes, to come here and show your undying loyalty. And we appreciate every single one of you for that. Unfortunately, not everyone will be admitted. Therefore, we have the physical examination. Today, you will prove your strength and endurance for your country. You will have to run five miles, carry a hundred pounds for a mile, swim 500 yards and other exercises to prove you are fit for the Tatmadaw. Please follow my assistant to the shed. There, you will be given proper clothing, water, food and anything else you might need. I will be timing each and every one of you. Those who aren't able to complete the tasks or finish in the last three will be dismissed." He nods toward his assistant. "Take them away."

Everyone follows the stick-like man to the huge shed and each of you is given a pair of active clothes. When you reach the station, you're given a short-sleeved shirt and shorts.

The assistant man points to the bathroom. You mutter thank you but by the time you look back, he's already done with the next person.

You enter the bathroom and tug the new clothes on. They're light as if you're covered by clouds.

Thud. Thud.

"Hurry up in there," a gruff voice commands. You throw open the door.

You glare at the giant in front of you.

He furrows his eyebrows. "You got a problem?"

Your mouth stretches into a frown. "No."

"Thought so." The giant enters the stall you were in. You shake your head and make your way toward everyone else.

"I've been preparing for this for the past two decades. This'll be easy," a scrawny man boasts, a crowd gathering around him.

Some of the spectators roll their eyes toward him while others drool with awe. You, it just reactivates my nerves. You look down and gulp hard.

"You'll be fine," you try to reassure yourself but it does nothing.

CHAPTER 29

TAREK

I WATCH AS he turns toward me, his mouth moving. I blink a few times and focus.

"What are you looking at?" the soldier asks, inching toward me.

"No—Nothing, sir."

"You were looking at me, right?"

Now, the soldier is in my face, his eyes piercing mine. His mouth is pulled back in a scowl.

I jerk back before Grandpa throws himself between the two of us.

"Get out of the way," he bellows but Grandpa doesn't move.

"My grandson didn't mean it like that, sir. He's just a child. You know how children are. Please forgive him."

"I said *move.*" The soldier shoves Grandpa. Grandpa grunts but holds his ground.

Within a split second, the soldier is on top of Grandpa, his fist moving up and down.

Time slows down, and it's as if I'm walking on clouds. I barrel into the soldier, pinning him to the ground. His fist meets my jaw, and the force sends me down.

The soldier rolls on top of me, his anger shadowing the sun's light.

Smack. Smack. Smack.

Pain flashes through my face but my arms refuse to block them. They're glued to the ground. I try to lift them but they fall back down. I lay there, limp, waiting for another blow...

But it doesn't come.

The weight on my ribs evaporates. I open my eyes. The soldier stands next to me, his eyes focused far away.

"You know the commander told us to cut down on *activity* until the news gets off us, right?" a voice calls.

The soldier scowls and then turns to me.

Thud.

He buries his foot into my stomach and I crumple, gripping my aching stomach.

When I open my eyes, the soldier's gone.

Grandpa rushes over to me, rolling me over. "Tarek. Tarek. Are you okay?"

I sit up, ignoring the pain as I inhale. "I'm fine. Are you..." My words trail as I see the blood trickling from his mouth.

He smiles, forcing his mouth closed. "I'm fine. I'm fine."

I struggle to my feet, trying to hide the pain. The cart begins to rattle behind me as we walk toward home. The sun is inching toward its bed, the sky still a bright blue. A thick layer of clouds races toward the light, quickly covering the land in shadows.

"It'll rain tonight," Grandpa remarks when we get home.

CHAPTER 30

KAN

"ALRIGHT, EVERYONE," THE assistant announces. "Back to the platform."

The sea of young faces flows back where they came from. The commander remains still on his raised platform.

"Now that everyone has changed, it's time for forming groups. Everyone will divide themselves into groups of fifteen and make their way to one of the group leaders." He points toward the line of stiff adults. "Each group will start with a different test and will make their way through all the others. Understand?"

Everyone nods but your head remains frozen with nervousness. The flood of people pulls in different directions, the sea of arms tugging on anyone they can get their hands on.

An iron hand clasps itself onto your arm and you barrel forward. After a few minutes, the commotion dies down and you find yourself in a group of muscular recruits. You gulp as they brag about their skills.

"Seems like one of us isn't going to be able to make it," one of them says, his eyes piercing yours.

The others laugh and you can feel the heat spreading across your face.

"We'll see about that," you murmur.

The jock turns around. "What was that?"

"Nothing," you respond. He scowls at you but doesn't push you.

"Let's go," your group supervisor says and you follow him into a building.

Inside, the smell of chlorine slaps your nose. The clear, blue light illuminates the massive room.

"Alright, everyone, get in a lane."

You pick the corner one, trying to stay as far away from everyone as possible.

"You will swim ten laps. That means that you go to the end and come back. That's one lap. Ten of those. I'll be timing every one of you. Take your positions," he commands.

You position myself in a diving position above the edge of the pool.

You've got this. This is exactly like you practiced. It's nothing different.

"Three."

You shake the tension in your shoulders.

"Two."

You set your eyes on your target.

"One."

You take a deep breath.

"Go."

.   .   .

By the time you finish all ten laps, you collapse onto the floor. You lay on your back, trying to calm your panting chest.

The supervisor makes his way toward you, peering into your eyes. You immediately jump up.

"Great job, Kan. You're the first one to finish," he pats your shoulder.

You glance toward the lanes to see everyone else still in the water. You nod toward the supervisor.

"You can sit over there until it's time for the next exercise."

.   .   .

Toward the end of the day, your legs and arms are aching but you force yourself toward the platform. You finished first in every single exercise, all of them except the running with weights. You were the second last one to finish.

You can see your dreams being crushed. If only you had trained harder. If only you had practiced more. Now, you might not even make it into the Tatmadaw. You might have to go home and work as a shop owner or something else. You might have to give up on your dreams.

"Congratulations, everyone. You have made it through the physical examination. Get a good night's sleep and once you wake up, the results will be posted. If you did not make it, please make arrangements to return home. Thank you all for your dedication."

CHAPTER 31

TAREK

AS SOON AS we open the door, the bustling energy bursts through the house. I look toward Grandpa and he shrugs.

"Assalam Alaikum," we announce as the door shuts behind us.

"Walaikum Salam," Grandma and Mama reply, the hustle in their voices radiating.

"Is everything alright?" I ask as we enter the kitchen. Haya is on the floor, eating an apple happily as if the commotion is in our imaginations.

Mama pauses for a second. "Tomorrow is—*What happened?*"

I try to smile, but it comes out lopsided. Grandma turns toward us, her usual smile fading away. She rushes into the kitchen, coming out with a wet cloth. She holds it against Grandpa's bleeding mouth.

He takes it from her and squeezes her shoulder. He turns toward Mama. "Don't worry about it. What's going on here?"

Mama opens her mouth and then closes it. She looks at me, then Grandpa, and then back at me. She sighs. "We'll talk about this later. Tomorrow's Saturday."

I search my mind for anything. "So?" I ask.

Grandma sighs. "Tomorrow is when the regulators will come over here."

My eyes widen.

"We need to hide Harsa. The problem is we have nowhere she can stay. She'll need to go out for a few hours," Mama explains.

"But what if they find her?" Grandpa asks.

"They won't," Grandma reassures, "They won't."

"What can we do to help?" I ask.

"We need to hide everything of hers in case they search the house. We need to make sure there's no trace of her here," Mama says.

Grandpa and I nod.

. . .

"Hurry up. It's almost two o'clock," Grandpa calls out.

I rush to the front door. Uncle taps his foot against the floor, as if counting the seconds.

"Ali, we're leaving in one minute," Uncle booms, his deep voice rattling the house.

From our room, the sound of hurried footsteps echoes. The door flies open and Ali emerges, wearing a new gray shirt.

"We're going to be late," Grandpa mutters. "We're leaving now. We'll be back within an hour."

"Alright," Grandma responds from the kitchen, "Assalam Alaikum."

"Walaikum Salam," I call out before the door closes.

Grandpa speedwalks deep into the village and we struggle to keep up with him.

Ali staggers behind us. I tug on his arm. "Next time, don't take three hours."

He pouts. "It's not my fault."

"Whose is it then?" I ask.

"My clothes. They refused to iron," he responds.

"Sure, it was your clothes. Definitely not you who should have ironed them on time." I shake my head, smiling at his excuse. Grandpa takes a right before the market, heading toward the outskirts of the village.

I watch as the wood houses around us turn into quick blurs, morphing into one another. Dust flies into my shoe and I force myself to ignore it.

Uncle stops abruptly in front of an average-looking house. It looks just like ours. A one-story wooden house with a red roof.

Grandpa steps forward, reaching out to knock on the door but it swings open. A man, a few years younger than Grandpa, stands in the doorway. He smiles when he sees us.

"Welcome, Ayub. We were just about to get started," he says, his voice soft.

Uncle chuckles. "I'm glad you didn't."

We step inside the modest house.

.   .   .

I sit on the mat. Everyone around me greets each other. Hands clasp, arms wrap around each other, and the familiar sound of laughter echoes in the house.

"If everyone would please exit as soon as possible to ensure safety. There might be soldiers nearby and we don't want to alert them to our mosque. Please, a few at a time and in different directions to avoid looking suspicious," Hasan, the owner of the house, announces.

Some people nod and make their way toward the door. Others are still talking. Soon, Hasan is busy with everyone else, hurrying people out.

"Let's go. We don't want the soldiers to catch us praying Jumu'ah," Grandpa says.

Ali frowns and waves to one of his friends. We all gather near the door. Uncle turns the doorknob and we walk into the light.

We exit the house, making sure no one outside sees us. The last time a soldier caught us praying, they burned the house right there and then, killing everyone inside.

I shudder at the thought.

CHAPTER 32

KAN

AS SOON AS they dismiss you, all you want is to melt onto the floor. Your legs are like the ocean, threatening to sway at any second. Your lungs beg for air and your mouth is dry.

Your head pounds. You grip it, trying not to pass out.

The commander steps onto the platform again. "I forgot to mention that your group leaders will show you to your rooms. Please note that these are temporary dorms and will be switched if you're accepted into the academy."

The candidates pull in different directions. You drag yourself to your group leader, trying to wipe the sickness from your face.

Everyone in your group looks greenish. Their eyes are barely open and they're slouching. Some grip their stomachs while others try not to wobble.

"Follow me," the leader says and turns. You force yourself to walk.

One step.

Two steps.

Three steps.

After a few minutes, he stops and everyone clamors around him. Your vision crisps to a modern hallway. The floor is made of marble tiles and large doors line the hallway.

"Divide yourselves into groups of two. Each group will take one room," the leader orders.

Instantly, people tug on their friends and form groups. Only you and one other person are left. You shrug your shoulders and stand next to him.

The leader walks around, handing each group a set of keys. "Each set has a number. That's your room number," he explains.

The cool metal keys weigh down in your hand. Your hand barely wraps around one of them.

"Have a good night's sleep, everyone," the leader says before turning and walking down the hall.

As soon as he's out of sight, everyone dashes toward their room.

Click.

The door throws itself open once you turn the key. You don't think after that. You toss your bags on the ground and collapse onto the bed, embracing the darkness.

CHAPTER 33

TAREK

BY THE TIME the moon rises, all of Aunt's belongings are hidden. Mama puts the brick back where it belongs. Inside a hole in the wall, all of Aunt's clothes, hijabs and books lay in the shadows. We do a few rounds around the house, just in case.

Everyone retreats to their rooms after. I step into the kitchen to find Haya asleep on the floor, her empty plate in front of her. I wash her dish, pick her up, and lay her down in Mama's room.

·   ·   ·

As soon as I tumble off my bed, my eyes crack wide open. Ali isn't in his bed, the door cracked slightly open.

I stretch my tight arms and legs and roll out of my blanket, snatching my clothes from the side.

Opening the door, I rub my eyes, glancing out the window. The sky outside is streaked with light pink on top of dark blue. The trees outside are dotted with sparkling drops and the ground is dark brown compared to its usual dusty brown.

"Tarek? Hurry up. They'll be here any minute," Mama calls.

"Yes, Mama," I respond in a deep, sleepy voice.

I wash up in the bathroom and exit within a few minutes. Outside, everyone is seated in the living room.

Everyone except Aunt.

"She's near the river, hiding out. She'll be back in a few hours," Uncle explains, reading my mind.

We sit in silence, waiting for the inevitable knock.

Thud. Thud.

The door thunders as two heavy fists beat it. Grandpa walks up and throws the door wide open.

"Welcome," he says, but the two men brush him aside. They storm into the house. One holds up a clipboard.

"Everyone, stand in a line," the taller one gruffs. He's wearing a dark green suit with a red badge on the left shoulder.

The other is wearing the exact same thing but holds a clipboard, tapping the pen against it. We all form a line.

The taller one steps into Uncle's face. "Name?"

"Yusuf Asad," Uncle says, loud and clear.

The clipboard man scratches something on the board.

"Name?" the taller one asks Grandpa.

"Ayub Asad."

Again, the clipboard man writes something down.

The taller man continues down the line until he reaches me.

"Name?" he booms, his nose almost reaching my eyes. I force myself not to jerk backward.

"Tarek Asad," I reply.

He grunts.

A few seconds later, the taller one towers over the clipboard man's shoulder. They stand there for a few minutes, their eyes speaking.

We don't dare move.

"Is there anyone else in the house?" The clipboard man asks, his voice thin and scratchy.

"No, sir," Grandpa responds firmly.

He nods and then puts his board down. Both men separate, heading in different directions. From inside the rooms, we listen as drawers are flipped upside down, closets are rummaged through, and beds are moved.

But we still don't dare to move.

"Alright, looks fine," the taller man yells toward the clipboard man.

Without a single word, the door slams shut, mirroring the drop in my heartbeat.

"The small one had a funny nose," Haya laughs, but her voice becomes muffled. We turn toward Haya to find Mama covering her mouth.

"Shhhh," she scolds.

Haya instantly grows quiet, a blanket of embarrassment covering her eyes.

Grandpa and Grandma collapse on the floor cushions, relieved. Uncle paces the room.

"Sit down, Yusuf," Mama says.

"Not until Harsa comes back," he says, still walking in circles.

Mama sighs and dismisses him. A shadow casts over her face. The same thing happened with Papa. He didn't come back from work one day, and Mama refused to eat or sleep until he came back. She thought that maybe he stayed at work for longer.

He never did.

We got the letter later stating that Papa was an enemy of the state and would be promptly executed. Mama has never been the same since.

I glance over toward her to see the flash of a tear in her eye before it's sucked back in.

CHAPTER 34

KAN

AS SOON AS the sun peeks out from the horizon, you're up and out of the room. You didn't sleep much due to your anticipation, a mix of excitement and worry. Now, it's finally time to see if your dreams have come true.

You crack open the door slowly, glancing behind to see if your roommate has woken up.

As soon as the door clicks in place, you dash to the end of the hall, where the wall is plastered with paper. You scan for your name.

Aung Kan.

You move your finger across the bar.

Accepted.

"Yahoo," you scream out and instantly slap your mouth. You listen carefully for any sound, but only the echoes of snoring resonate throughout the hall. You jump up and down.

You got in. You got in. You're a soldier. Your dream has come true.

You skip throughout the dorms in your own world. You daydream about the future, watching as you protect your country. You picture yourself around a campfire, telling scary stories to your fellow soldiers.

This is the life you've dreamed of.

You whip your phone out of your pocket and click furiously. You place it against your ear as the dial tone rings in your ear.

"Hello?" Mama's voice says.

"Mama, I got in. I'm a soldier now," you exclaim.

"I knew you could do it," she responds, joy woven in her voice. "I'm so proud of you."

Creeeaak.

A few other recruits creep out of their rooms, each making their way to the posters.

"Okay, Mama. I have to go now. I'll talk to you later."

"Alright. I love you."

"I love you too."

Click.

The call hangs up, and I place my phone back in my pocket. A dorm supervisor makes his way to the seat near the posters.

Crack.

"It's five o'clock. Check if you've been accepted into the Tatmadaw. If not, please arrange to return home. For those of you who have accepted, take today off and get to know your peers. Training begins tomorrow," the man in the intercom announces.

A few of the young men's faces hang low and they walk back to their dorms with slouched backs. Others celebrate, their arms wrapped around their friends. Their laughter rings throughout the halls and the dorm supervisor smiles.

You smile with them.

A finger taps on your shoulders. You turn around to find a small man, his head at your chin, looking up at you. His head shines in the light, small buds of hair sprouting out.

"Hello," he says, and smiles a toothy grin at you.

"Hi," you respond.

"I'm Bennu."

"I'm Kan. Nice to meet you."

"You don't look like you know anyone around here."

You nod.

"Come on. I'll introduce you to my friends. The more the merrier."

Bennu grabs your wrist and pulls you toward a group of three other men.

"Guys, this is Kan. He doesn't know anyone around here, so I thought he could be the fourth member of our group."

"I'm Htun," a tall, boney man with black, rectangular glasses says. A few red pimples are scattered on his forehead.

"I'm Cetan," a boy who is a copy of Bennu says.

"We're twins," Bennu says and slings his arm around Cetan's shoulders.

"It's nice to meet you," you say, smiling.

"Come on. Sit down with us," Cetan says, patting to the empty space beside him.

You take a seat, relishing the friendly air.

CHAPTER 35

TAREK

TAP. TAP.

The gentle knocking on the door turns into the *creak* of it opening. Aunt peeps her head in, searching the house for strangers.

As soon as Uncle sees her, his eyes light up, and he stands up. Both of them embrace. I glance toward Mama and watch her heavy, soft eyes. If only she and Papa were reunited.

Mama catches me staring at her and she smiles, trying to hide the pain in her eyes. I smile back.

"Grandpa, shouldn't we go to work?" Ali asks.

Grandpa shakes his head. "Not today. Everyone will stay at home due to the regulators' visitors. We'll take a break today."

Uncle and Ali nod, a sigh of relief escaping Uncle's lips.

Mama heads to her room, followed by Grandma. Grandpa retreats to his room. "I'm going to take a nap. I barely slept last night."

"We're going for a walk," Uncle announces and tugs on Aunt's hand. The door closes behind them.

Ali gets up and goes to our room, leaving me and Haya in the living room.

"Want to make dinner early and then play?" I ask her. Haya's face lights up and she nods.

. . .

Hours later, dinner is set on the floor.

"Let's go get everyone else," I grunt as I lift Haya off the counter. A few minutes later, all of us are seated, the pot in front of us steaming. Everyone is smiling as if the morning's events had never occurred. As if it's a brand-new day.

"Looks really good, Tarek," Grandma says, and everyone nods.

"We'll have to see how it tastes, though," Ali chuckles.

Everyone laughs, the white of their teeth illuminating the kitchen. The clatter of spoons against the clay plates rings throughout the room. Within minutes, the food is gone and I pile the dishes in the sink. I scan the kitchen around me and glance back at Haya.

"We've got some cleaning to do."

.   .   .

My eyes jerk open before the sun is up. Outside, the black sky is streaked with blue with the stars speckled all over. I tiptoe out of the room, Ali's snores ringing in my ear.

I crack open the newspaper.

Regulations in the Rakhine State are successful.

A white rectangle floats down from within the paper. I pick it up.

To Harsa Asad.

I place the envelope on the kitchen counter and go to the bathroom.

.   .   .

I tap my pencil against the floor, waiting for something, anything, to happen. It's been hours since I've been awake and the usual sound of laughter and Haya's playful screams are locked away. Instead, a heavy silence hangs in the house.

I stare at my geometry book, the numbers and letters morphing into cackling blurs. My mind refuses to comprehend anymore.

Kr. Kr.

The pages land on each other softly and the cover plops onto them. I rest my head against the wall for a few seconds.

I walk to the kitchen to check the time.

7:13 a.m.

A lightbulb shines on top of my head as a mischievous smile spreads across my face. I crack open our room's door, peeking inside. Ali is still snoring.

I grab a pot and wooden spoon and tiptoe near his head. I place the pot near his head and steady myself.

"One, two, three," I whisper and *crash,* I slam the spoon into the pot. Ali jerks awake, screaming. As soon as his fingers grab the pot, I make a run for it.

Ali grunts in anger and darts toward me. He jumps onto me, me still laughing. He pins my arms under his knees.

"Ow, ow," I say as I continue laughing. Tears stream down my face and the air around us grows warm.

Creeeak.

A foot sticks out from the room and Aunt gently closes the door behind her. She freezes when she sees an angry Ali on top of a hysterical me.

"Uhhh?" she says as a smile spreads on her face. Ali's face softens.

"You have a letter on the counter," I wheeze after I calm down.

Aunt nods and steps over us. I watch as Ali's face morphs from the softness to raw fury.

"What is wrong with you?" he spits.

"Come on, you were supposed to wake up anyway," I respond.

"Not like that, though." He grabs the pot and spoon from beside us and places it on my head.

Bang. Bang. Bang.

He hits the pot hard, and it trembles, rattling my brain. After a couple of hits, he takes it off. My fuzzy vision watches as he calms down.

He hoists me up, holding me up as I grip my pounding head.

"I'm sorry," he says softly and I nod, even though everything hurts.

"Are you okay?" he asks.

"Yeah," I respond, even though I can't hear him properly.

"Tarek?" Aunt calls from the kitchen.

Ali responds for me, "Yes?"

"Where'd you get this from?"

"Newspaper," I mumble incoherently.

"In the newspaper," Ali repeats.

Aunt emerges from the kitchen, her face a ghostly white.

CHAPTER 36

KAN

YOU ROLL OVER in your bed, your eyes fluttering open. You stretch, making sure not to wake your roommates.

Last night was the most fun you've ever had. You made three friends, and you spent the night singing, dancing and partying.

Of course, you didn't drink any alcohol. Just the thought of it makes you sick.

Hatred burns in your stomach as your father creeps into your mind. He was a drunkard. Every morning, he would come back home completely wasted, murmuring and giggling as if nothing had happened. After he sobered up, he would cry and beg Mama for forgiveness only to do the same thing again.

And again.

And again.

Until one day, he didn't even come back home. The police knocked on the door one morning.

"Good morning, ma'am. Are you Maung Thet's wife?"

"Yes?" Mama responded. "What is this about?"

"Your husband," the officer responded, a sullen look in his eyes.

Mama signaled for me to go to my room. I rushed there but peered outside, curious.

"Is he dead?" Mama asked quietly.

The officer shook his head. "He was in a severe accident. He's at the hospital right now but...he won't be returning home, ma'am."

I watch as he hands Mama a piece of paper.

"He was the one responsible for the accident and he killed the other passenger. He was also found extremely drunk. He will be swiftly tried and convicted."

Mama stared at the paper.

"I'm so sorry, ma'am," the officer said.

She swallowed hard. "Can I offer you anything? Tea? Cookies? Fruit?" she peeped.

The officer smiled sadly. "No, thank you. Have a great day."

And with that, he left.

You haven't seen Father ever since.

You rest your head on your hand as you go through the years after. Instantly, you jerk your hand away and sniff yourself.

You celebrated a little too much. You jump out of bed and grab your uniform, leaving the room to shower.

The hallways are empty except for the occasional security guard. You rush toward the showers but freeze when you see the commander in the hallways.

You duck behind the hall.

"Kan?" the commander calls.

You straighten yourself up and appear before him. "Yes, sir?"

"You're awake before the rest of your peers," he states.

You nod.

"Your group supervisor told me about you two days ago. He said you did incredibly well, coming first in all but one of the exercises. You even managed to do extra by swimming another four laps."

He scans you. "I see you have a lot of potential in you. I can see you as a general, or at least a commander in the future."

You smile sheepishly.

"But that's if you focus. Don't lose sight of your goals and don't get distracted. Everyone will want to be your friend when they see you becoming successful, but they're only trying to snatch that glory away from you. Be careful how and who you spend your time with."

He reaches forward and pats your shoulder. "I hope to see you up there in the future."

The commander's footsteps grow quiet but you remain frozen in place.

Was he warning you about Bennu, Cetan, and Htun? Or was he warning you about everyone?

For some reason, a chill runs down your spine and you glance over your shoulder before you dart for the showers.

CHAPTER 37

TAREK

ALI SHOOTS OFF me, instantly going to Aunt. I'm slower and I painfully make my way to her.

"What's wrong?" Both of us ask.

"Nothing, nothing," she reassures, but the fear in her eyes says otherwise. "Get back to what you were doing."

Ali turns toward me with puzzled eyes.

Creak. Thud.

The sound of the house waking up snaps our eyes away from each other. Grandpa and Grandma come out from rooms and Mama and Uncle open their doors. All of them freeze when they see Aunt.

Uncle makes his way toward his wife.

"Is everything alright?" Grandpa asks.

Aunt shakes her head, holding out the opened letter. Uncle's eyes scan the paper and his face turns pale.

"Read it out loud," Grandpa says.

"To Harsa Asad. We have been informed that you attempted to evade the population regulators that arrived at your house a few days ago. For breaking the law, you have two days to pack and leave the country. If you try to evade us again, please note that the punishment is execution. If we find you trying to enter the country after exile, you will also be executed."

As the words process in our minds, deadly silence snakes its way into the house. No one dares to move, instead standing with their mouths hanging open.

Uncle begins to tremble, red taking over his eyes. "We should've taken the picture again."

"How? We couldn't afford it." Aunt says, desperately.

"We could've sold something. We could've asked a neighbor. We could have done something."

Aunt reaches for Uncle's shoulder. "It's alright."

"No, it's not. I should have insisted on retaking the picture."

"There's nothing we could have done," Aunt responds gently.

"But we could've done *something*. Why didn't you beg us for a retake? Why did you give in?"

"I didn't know this was going to happen," Aunt bursts.

We let them go back and forth as smoke clouds the two of them. No one moves. No one says anything. We just stand there, feet glued to the floor.

.   .   .

Aunt and Uncle spend the rest of their day in their room, the occasional hum of whispering coming from there. The rest of us continue our days silently. Haya is oblivious to what happened in the morning, still trying to goof around. Her laughter echoes throughout the stiff air.

"Tarek, play with me," she begs.

I shake my head.

"Why? You've been studying all day," she complains.

I don't say anything. She continues talking, but it goes straight through my ears. The only thing I can hear is Uncle's strained voice reading the letter.

.   .   .

The next morning is the same as yesterday. Complete silence.

At about noon, Aunt and Uncle emerge from their room, two bags slung on Aunt's shoulders.

They make their way to the front door and Aunt sets her bags down. We make our way to the door, blankly staring at the bags.

"What's going on?" Haya asks.

Mama scoops her up.

"Aunt's going away for a little while," she whispers.

"Why?" Haya asks.

"For business." Mama attempts to smile but barely musters a weak one.

I glance toward Uncle, whose face is still pale and empty. The hollow, dark circles under his eyes are more apparent than usual.

"It's time for goodbye," Aunt whispers, "I'm sorry for causing this. I really am. I..." her eyes dart toward Haya. "This shouldn't have happened. I'm sorry."

Aunt's eyes flood but she wipes her tears away. A glistening bead of crystal water drips down Uncle's cheek. Grandma wraps Aunt in a hug.

"Maybe one day, we'll reunite somewhere out of this country," she offers with a hopeful voice.

"Don't worry. I'll be back soon," Aunt responds.

Uncle freezes. "Don't. Don't try to come back. You know what will happen."

Aunt doesn't respond and hugs Mama next. A few minutes later, the door closes, the *thud* echoing through the heavy air.

CHAPTER 38

KAN

"ALRIGHT EVERYONE. You're dismissed for lunch," Sayar Nay announces after glancing down at his watch.

The second the word *lunch* comes out of his mouth, everyone floods out of the room, carrying you with them. You spot Bennu and the rest of the group walking toward the cafeteria and you duck into the bathroom.

You wait inside until the commotion outside dies down. You scan the hallways for Cetan, Htun or Bennu but you don't see any of them. Within seconds, the apple you had in your bag is devoured. You throw the core away and walk in the hall.

"Kan? Kan."

You force yourself not to look over your shoulder and you stick your hands into your pockets.

"Kan?" A hand turns your around. You stare into Bennu's eyes.

"Why were you ignoring me?" he asks, concern in his eyes.

"I didn't hear you," you lie.

"Yeah right. There's no noise here. I would hear a pin drop in here. How could you have not heard me?"

"I just didn't hear you, okay?" You mutter and push past him.

He tugs you back again. "What's wrong? Did we do something wrong? Did *I* do something wrong?"

"No, no."

"Did something happen to your family? Are you sick?"

You shake your head. "Please leave me alone."

"I won't. What's wrong?"

"It's nothing," you say, "It's really nothing."

"Why didn't you sit with us? Why are you walking by yourself?"

You think of the best excuse you can. "I want to be alone."

"On the second day of being here and when nothing's wrong. Come on, tell me," he pleads.

You groan and give in. "It's just that...that...you know."

He listens attentively.

"I don't know. The commander told me to focus on my studies and not get carried away with friends and stuff, you know. I thought I should—"

"Take his advice?" Bennu interrupts.

You nod.

"Kan, I understand why you would do that. The commander knows what he's doing and you want to be like him. We all do. Believe me. We all want to be successful and flourish in the army. But at the same time, there has to be a balance. We can't be all disciplined and focused. We need to have some fun too."

You nod. You knew he would say that.

"Come on. Let's go back to Cetan and Htun. They might worry. We're trying to plan to go out on the weekend. It'll be fun," he says, trying to entice you to come with him.

You let him grab your hand and pull you into the mass of noise inside the cafeteria.

CHAPTER 39

TAREK

THE SECOND AUNT leaves, the tears start. Mama and Grandma retreat to Mama's room. Grandpa goes to his room and Uncle, Uncle collapses onto the floor cushions, blankly staring at the wall.

I sit down next to him and put my hand on his shoulder.

"Uncle?"

He doesn't respond.

"Uncle?"

He slowly turns his head toward me. He gets up. "She couldn't have gotten that far, right? I'm going with her," he announces and darts toward the door.

"No." I tackle him.

He claws at me, his eyes crazed and red. "Let me go, Tarek. Let me go to her."

Grandpa and Mama burst out of their rooms.

"Please. I can catch up to her," Uncle cries, "Please."

He pushes me off him and reaches for the door handle. I barrel into him and Ali holds his arms down.

"Please. Please."

I glance up to see Haya at Mama's door, tears flooding her eyes. "Go inside," I command and she obeys, closing the door behind her.

Uncle stops struggling. "Please," he whispers.

Grandpa kneels down next to Uncle. "You can't. The border police will kill you. Aunt has a special pass in the system. They'll let her out but you don't. You'll die."

"I'll find a way. There's always a way," Uncle screams hysterically.

"No, you won't. We can't have another member of the family die," Grandpa says firmly.

"No, no, no," Uncle cries.

Grandpa hoists him up. "Let's go."

Uncle continues to cry, wailing like a toddler. His face turns bright red, and he reaches up toward his hair. His fingers interlace in the bush of hair and he tugs. Grandpa rips his hands off.

"Stop," he says gently and loops Uncle's arm onto his shoulder.

He walks him toward his room. He passes by ghostly Mama and he nods to her. "Don't worry about him. Give him some time," he reassures her.

She glances down toward the bent, limp figure of Uncle and she opens her mouth to say something.

Nothing comes out.

"He'll get better. He just needs some time," Grandpa affirms.

Grandma puts her hands on Mama's shoulders and Mama begins to weep. She digs her face into Grandma's shoulders.

"Shh. Shhh," Grandma says, rubbing Mama's back. There are tears in her eyes as well.

I gulp the boulder in my throat and proceed to Mama's room. As I pass Uncle's room, the sound of sobbing reaches my ear.

I try to shake it off as I open the door. Inside, Haya hides under a blanket. I sit down next to her and she peeks out from under.

"You can come out," I say.

She carefully emerges, her eyes darting throughout the room as if searching for something. Her eyes calm down after a few seconds and she jumps into my lap, wrapping her tiny arms around my waist. Haya digs her face into my stomach and a tingling sensation erupts from there.

I peel her face away from my stomach. "That tickles," I laugh.

As soon as I see her darkened face, I immediately hush. She rests her face down, not in my stomach this time.

"What's wrong?" I ask.

Her eyes sparkle, the tears threatening to pour out.

"Shh, no need to cry," I say as I hug her.

She stands on my leg and wraps her arms under my armpits, resting her head on my shoulder. Just like a baby.

"What's wrong?" I ask again, rubbing her back.

"Why was Uncle crying?" she whispers.

"He's sad that Aunt isn't here."

"When is she going to come back?"

I hesitate. "I don't know."

"Is she gone forever?" Haya asks with a slight hiccup.

"No, no," I respond instantly, even though I know that isn't the truth.

CHAPTER 40

KAN

"THERE YOU BOTH are," Cetan announces and Htun immediately turns to look behind him.

"Where were you?" Both of them ask.

"Our friend here wasn't sure if he was ready for the amount of fun we will be having," Bennu smiles. You turn away from him.

"Anyway, what time do you guys want to go out on Saturday?" Cetan asks.

Everyone looks toward you. "What time do you think would be best?"

You shrug your shoulders but they continue to stare at you. You have to answer them.

"Maybe sometime in the evening. That way, it would be cooler and if any of us have to run errands, we could finish them in the morning," you respond.

Bennu nods. "That sounds good. Does six o'clock work for everyone?"

Everyone nods. "Good. So what should we do?" Htun asks.

"How about we take it easy and wander the marketplaces? We could buy some stuff but also enjoy ourselves."

"Ooooo, we could eat street food," Htun says, licking his lips.

Bennu rolls his eyes. "Always about food with you. So is everyone good with the plan?"

Everyone nods and even though you don't want to, you can't help but savor the bubble of warmth inside of you.

. . .

Lunch passes by quickly. You don't even check your watch.

Htun checks his phone and notices the time. He and Cetan get up. "Alright guys. It's time to go back for training. Don't forget about Saturday's plan."

Bennu nods his head toward the exit. "Time for us to go back too. We have the special training course they released last year and I'm excited."

You nod. "Me too."

Both of you make your way to the right hallway and you enter the large lecture hall. You follow Bennu up to the middle of the seats and take a seat. On the projector, there's a blue slideshow labeled,

Intro to the Ethnic Composition of Myanmar

You glance toward Bennu and he rubs his hands together. "Seems interesting," he says.

There's something different in his eyes. Something hard and fiery. Not the usual softness in his eyes.

You snatch your notebook from your satchel and crack it open to a crisp new page. You sit attentively, waiting for the sound of words.

"Good morning class. I'm your professor, Sayar Zaw. I hope you all have had a productive day today. I know this is the first day of training but we still have some learning to do. Now, this is a less traditional class. We won't be talking about the different kinds of weapons or military tactics. This has more to do with the social structure in Myanmar. As you all know, there is one superior race here: the Bamar. Every single one of you is Bamar, or else you wouldn't be here. However, obviously, there are more than one race throughout the world."

He clicks on his computer and a map of Myanmar pops up. "That is how Myanmar is divided up. Each state is divided up based on the race or ethnicity of its inhabitants."

You lean forward, as if expecting the screen to draw you in. Sayar Zaw taps the screen with his pointer.

"*This,* this is the Rakhine State, the state with the most amount of trouble. We would have been a peaceful country had it not been for them. The Rohingya, those who reside in Rakhine, are not even similar to us Bamar. They are dark-skinned, with the ugliest facial features that make them look like trolls. That's exactly what they are: trolls.

"As you all know, Islam is a violent religion and the Rohingya practice it. They pray for our downfall *five* times a day. They aren't thankful for all the opportunities we have provided for them and they never will be.

"This is why we have this class. Someday, when the Rohingya attack, we need to be prepared. We need to be ready when they come for us. That time is coming soon. I can feel it."

CHAPTER 41

TAREK

I PICK HAYA up from my shoulder and place her down on the cot. I roll the blanket up to her chin and close the curtains. The streaks on her cheeks glisten as the sun's rays disappear.

I close the door behind me. Outside, Grandpa sits on a cushion and gestures for me to sit down next to him.

I grunt as I relax against the pillows.

"Tarek? I need to ask you something," Grandpa says.

"Hm?"

"You know your uncle won't be coming to work for a while, right?"

I nod. I know where this is going.

"That means I will need help with the shop. Ali is a great help but he asked me for a few weeks off. He's tired, I suppose."

"I'll do it," I say, even though my heart begs to say no.

"Okay," Grandma whispers and then closes his eyes and reclines. We stay like that for a while, savoring the silence.

"Not today though. Today, I'm not going to work," he announces.

I nod. "Whenever you want to go, I'm ready."

.   .   .

The day passes by painfully. Each minute is an hour. Everyone is huddled in their rooms, crying or whispering. No one comes out to eat. No one comes out to go to the bathroom. It's as if ghosts have replaced the living, cheerful spirits. It's as if those living, cheerful spirits are now hollow, dead remains.

I shudder just thinking about death. The echoing of screams, begging and wailing outside is more prominent in the silence. The closing of curtains, the slams of doors and the whispers send shudders down my spine.

I force myself to get off the floor and go to the kitchen. The thought of food makes my stomach churn, even though it shrieks for attention.

I glance toward the clock.

8:03 p.m.

I snatch an apple from the counter and devour it. I cut another one into slices and place them in a bowl, making my way to Mama's room.

Tap. Tap.

I gently knock on the door to let Haya know I'm coming in. I step in and sit down next to her.

A storybook is cracked on her lap but her eyes are red and the pages are dotted with water.

I hand her the bowl and she gobbles the slices within a few seconds.

"Do you want anything else?" I ask.

She shakes her head.

"Alright. Get ready to sleep. You know what you have to do right?"

She nods. "Brush my teeth, change my clothes and wash my face," she says quietly.

I smile slightly. "I'll be in the living room if you need help."

"Can you sleep with me?"

I look back to her begging eyes and smile slightly. "As long as you finish getting ready on time."

. . .

As soon as I finish breakfast, Grandpa wakes up. "Ready to go?" he asks.

I nod.

"Give me a few minutes to eat something and then we'll go."

I grab a hat and wait outside, leaning against the cart. My fingers brush the history book's rough cover.

Creeeeeak.

The door screams open and Grandpa steps into the light.

"Same as last time, right?" I ask.

"The same," Grandpa responds.

I grip the handles and off we go.

.   .   .

Books aren't *just* books. They're ships on a river, waiting to carry you across. That's why you can get carried away, not noticing the change around you.

"Tarek? Tarek?" Grandpa calls out.

I rip my eyes off my history book. "Yes?"

He sighs and plops down next to me. "I see you brought your book with you."

I nod. I have to keep up with my studies while working too.

"Tarek, I—You can't read while working with me."

He pauses, waiting for an answer, but my lips are glued together.

"You have to focus on what you're doing. You're here to help, not sit while I do most of the work."

"I'm sorry, Grandpa," I mutter.

He smiles slightly. "Books are supposed to remain at home. That's where they belong. Just like your mind belongs to selling fish so we can have food on the table, understand?"

I nod and close the book, my tongue a sandy mass.

CHAPTER 42

TAREK

SATURDAY COMES WITHIN the blink of an eye and you find yourself wandering around campus, waiting for the clock to strike six.

By the time it's five thirty, you're at the double doors that lead outside. You pace in circles, trying to keep your excitement contained.

Bennu and Cetan arrive at 5:55 while Htun arrives exactly at six. Something inside you itches but you shove it away.

"Everyone ready to go?" Bennu asks, beaming.

You nod. "Alright, let's go then."

The four of you step out into the warm, still air of the outdoors. The retreating sunlight tickles your face and the bustle of crowds echoes throughout the town.

The group turns left and starts up toward a small hill. "The marketplace is over there," Cetan explains, directing his eyes toward you.

You nod, rubbing your fingers together. You don't know why but you feel...nervous. You try to bury the nervousness away.

Ten minutes later, you're standing at the entrance of the robust marketplace. Groups of teenagers bounce from window to window, their eyes bright. Couples smile with a few shopping bags in their arms. Some struggle to keep their children with them, one wandering here and the other going there.

Cetan elbows you. "Pretty nice, right?"

You nod, a smile growing on your face.

"Come on. What are we waiting for? The place to close?" Htun exclaims, jittery with excitement.

You all follow Htun through the shops, letting him pile bags of food samples on you all. Cetan rolls his eyes.

"Come on, isn't this enough? How much more do you want?" he whines with a smile.

"*This* is my definition of fun, alright? This and then exercising to make sure I don't gain weight," Htun says, crossing his arms.

"Alright, alright. Come on, let's go find somewhere to sit and try all these out," Bennu says.

You all sit down on a table next to a water fountain. You and Cetan lay out all the food and everyone digs in.

"Mmm, this one is great. We should get more of the *mont lone yay paw*," Htun says with his mouth full.

"First, chew with your mouth closed and *then* we'll get more." Cetan pokes him.

You laugh with everyone, finally cherishing the freedom you've waited so long for.

CHAPTER 43

TAREK

WE CONTINUE THE same routine for two weeks. Grandpa and I wake up and leave for work. By the time we come back, everyone is eating lunch. Everyone except for Uncle.

Every day, Mama gives me the same tired hello and every day, Grandma smiles sadly. She sits on the floor cushions, a pile of shirts by her side and a needle in her hand. The pile grows higher and higher, as if she is sewing her grief into the clothes.

"Can you sell these at your stall too?" she asks, handing me the pile.

I nod. She sits right back down and gets to work again.

I lock myself in the bathroom, gripping my head with my hands. My ribs have begun to show and the shadows under my eyes seem to droop down toward the Earth's center.

Haya is the only one who has recovered. She jumps onto me and hugs me tightly.

"Let's play now," she says every day.

And that's how each agonizing day passes by.

.   .   .

"Where's Haya?" I ask, stepping into the cool house. Grandpa has already taken a seat for lunch and Mama hands him some salad.

"Oh, she went outside. Some of the neighborhood kids were out and she wanted to play," Mama responds.

I shrug my shoulders and go into the kitchen to grab some fruit.

"How was your day?" Mama asks.

"Same as usual. Nothing out of the ordinary—"

Crash.

Both of us jump toward the kitchen entrance. Haya stands in the middle of the living room, bright red. Beads of glass drip down her cheeks and her eyes are cracked with red lines.

"Mama. *Mama,*" she screams.

Haya darts toward Mama and tugs on her hand. Mama lurches forward but holds her ground.

"Come on. Come on," she screams, pulling harder.

Mama resists. "What's wrong?" she screams even louder.

Haya peers at me for a split second and the next, she's dragging me. I scoop her up.

"What's wrong?" I ask, trying to keep myself calm, trying to keep my voice low.

"Aunt. It's Aunt," she wheezes as she pushes away from me. She smacks me in the face and my arms shoot up to grip my throbbing cheek. Haya grabs my hand again, dragging me behind her. This time, I let her. Mama and everyone else follow behind.

We travel farther and farther from the village, the green getting darker and darker. The road disappears and the crunch of grass rings in my ear. Sharp blades bite at my legs but Haya continues running. The blood pounding in my head gets hotter and hotter.

Haya jerks to a stop in front of a shallow pond, the stampede of footsteps behind us getting closer and closer.

She points toward a mass in the water. I float through the murky water, my feet barely touching the mossy ground. The water around me ripples as I inch toward the body. It's clearly a female, her dark hair spreading in the water beneath her. She's face down in the water. I shudder before flipping her over.

I yelp and fall backward, the sunlight turning into dark brown rays in the water. A pair of strong hands hoist me up. I gasp as I break the surface. I wipe the water from my eyes and stare at the body.

It's a woman in her mid-thirties with pale skin and rosy cheeks. Her amber eyes are wide open, blankly staring at the sky. Around her neck, a splash of blue claws at her neck.

It's Aunt.

My mouth turns into a desert and my heart beats in my throat. Beside me, Grandpa gasps. His hands tremble as he runs his fingers along her eyes, closing them.

Haya whimpers behind us and I glance over my shoulder. She buries her face in Mama's shirt. Mama's mouth hangs open while Grandma stands frozen, not blinking.

I turn to Grandpa and he swallows hard. He inches closer to the body. He crouches down, his hands swimming under his daughter-in-law's body and flips her over again. Her fear-stricken face disappears under the brown water.

"We can't touch the body. If the soldiers find out that we did...we'll all die," Grandpa whispers.

A hand squeezes my shoulder. "Come on," he whispers.

But I can't move.

It's as if the plants in the pond are wrapping around my feet, pulling me down.

My chest tightens and the surrounding air grows heavy.

Grandpa loops his arm in mine and pulls me away.

I try to say that I'm fine but it's as if a rock has clogged my throat. I let Grandpa pull me through the water. I let Grandma and Mama rip me out. I let all of them guide me back home, where Uncle awaits with a heavy, tear-stricken face.

CHAPTER 44

KAN

"COME ON GUYS, let's do something else. We've been eating for over fifteen minutes. I'm going to wander around if someone wants to come with," Cetan says while dramatically pushing his chair back.

"I'll come," Bennu says.

"Me too," you say.

"Wait for me," Htun exclaims and eats the last few crumbs on the table.

"Ew, who does that?" Cetan cringes.

Htun snorts and you chuckle. Soon, he joins the group.

"Where do you guys want to go now?" he asks.

You shrug your shoulders. "Wherever you all want."

"Let's explore the city. I can't even look at food right now," Cetan offers.

Everyone falls back so Cetan can lead the way. Soon, the hustle and bustle of the market is behind you and darkness swoops in. Only a few street lights illuminate the area.

Suddenly, Bennu stops. "Did you guys hear that?" he whispers.

You shake your head.

"Shh, listen," he says.

All of you stand perfectly still and the gentle sound of footsteps hitting the pavement rings near you.

"Someone's there," Htun shudders.

"No kidding," Cetan says.

Click.

You cover your eyes as a ball of light hurls itself at you. You gently open them back up when the flashlight is pointed in the opposite direction.

Sorry, Bennu mouths to you.

He sweeps the light around the area until it catches a shadow.

"It's a kid," Htun exclaims.

You blink a few times and the figure grows crisp. Instantly, your heart begins to pump faster.

The dark skin, the curly hair, the skeleton-like frame.

He's from the Rohingya.

The toddler covers his eyes and backs up into the shadows.

"You guys want to have some fun?" Cetan asks, a hint of slyness in his eyes.

Htun nods and you do too, having no idea what he means. Cetan nods toward Bennu.

"Hey, come here. We won't hurt you. Are you lost?" Bennu talks to the toddler gently.

He peeps his head from behind a box and nods.

"Come. I'll help you find your home." Bennu takes a step into the alley. The toddler hesitates but makes his way toward him.

As soon as he's within arm's reach, Bennu snatches him up and covers his mouth.

"Shhh, you wouldn't want something to happen to you, would you?" he whispers, his gentle eyes suddenly morphing into those of a fox.

Bennu gestures toward the boy in his arms. Htun and Cetan move in closer.

"You know what happens to illegal residents, right?" he asks us.

Htun grins slyly. "Of course"—he glances toward me—"we are soldiers now. It's our duty to make sure our country is rid of these varmints."

I glance over to Cetan, who is in his own world.

"Cetan? *Cetan?*" Bennu calls.

"Hm?"

"You know, you brought *something*." Bennu raises an eyebrow.

Cetan smiles and reaches for the boy's legs. He and Bennu stretch him out. You turn toward the boy. His eyes beg you, beg you to stop them. He tries to struggle but it only makes Bennu and Cetan's grip tighter. He thrashes his head from side to side, trying to free his mouth to scream.

That only makes your blood turn hot.

Look at him, helpless and alone, knowing he's in trouble. He shouldn't have been here if he wanted to avoid trouble. He belongs in any other country, just not Myanmar. These filthy things corrupt your country.

"Kan?"

You lock eyes with Cetan. "Yeah?"

"Can you grab the thing from my pocket? My hands are busy right now," he asks.

You nod and slip your hand in his pocket. Inside, there's a small knife, slightly bigger than your hand. On the handle, there's an intricate design carved into it. You run your hand along it, mesmerized by its beauty.

"Htun, care to do the honors?"

A large hand appears in front of you and you hand the knife over.

You look up to see a wild fire dancing in everyone's eyes. The glint of metal over Htun's head blinds you.

Splat. Splat. Splat.

CHAPTER 45

TAREK

AS SOON AS Mama tells Uncle about the news, he breaks down. He locks himself in his room and doesn't eat, go to the bathroom or move. All he does is sleep.

"We can't let him live like this," Mama says at dinner. "He's got to get out of his depression."

Grandpa shakes his head. "Let him for a little while. At least a month. Let him process this and he'll get over it soon."

The rest of dinner is spent in silence. I glance over to Haya's plate, which is untouched.

"Eat," I whisper as I nudge her.

"Mm mm." She shakes her head.

"Please."

She takes her spoon and takes one bite but that's it. She doesn't eat any more than that. I don't push her.

As soon as someone finishes, they wash their plates and go to their rooms. Soon, there's only me and Haya left.

"Come on," I say but as soon as she hears me, she bursts into tears. I lift her like a baby and pat her back, walking to Mama's room. I lay her down and hum until her eyes close.

.   .   .

Every morning, I wait by the cart. Every morning, Grandpa and I go to the river and fish. Every morning, we go to the market to sell fish.

And every morning, we witness the same oppression.

Burmese sellers refuse to sell anything to the Rohingya. The soldiers taunt us, sometimes smacking a passerby with the butt of his rifle. Sometimes, the echo of a scream silences the market, everyone frozen in place until the screams fade away.

Throughout the rest of the afternoon, Grandpa and I sell the rest of the fish. Both of us take opposite sides of the cart to maximize sales.

The trip back home is spent in silence and as we inch closer and closer to home, the air growing thick and heavy. I park the cart in the stall behind our house.

"Assalam Alaikum," I call out but no one responds. As I walk around the house, every single door is closed, the sound of whispering and weeping coming from inside every one of them.

I go back into the kitchen and grab a bowl, filling it with noodles. I fill a cup of water and put the two on a tray.

Knock. Knock.

No response.

"Uncle, can I come in?"

Still no response. I steady the tray on my arm and turn the knob. Inside, a mass lies in the bed, only a bush of hair showing from underneath.

I place the tray on the table next to the bed and sit on the edge.

"Come on, Uncle. You have to eat something or else. You'll die."

A small voice response from inside the blanket. "What's the point in living when they can come and snatch everything away from us? What's the point in living when everyone around you can disappear from your life?"

We sit in silence for a few seconds.

"At least eat a little bit. We don't want you to be taken away too. You're like this because one person has gone but what will we do if we lose you too?" I whisper.

Uncle slowly takes his blanket off and peers into my eyes. He nods slightly.

"Tell me when you're done. I'll pick up the tray," I say as I get up.

As soon as I close the door behind me, I hear the tears drip again.

CHAPTER 46

KAN

AS SOON AS your roommate closes the curtains, you see red.

All over the walls, all over the ceiling, all over the floor, there's a thick, dripping layer of red. It taunts you; it laughs at you, daring you to do anything.

You remain frozen, the red holding you down as it bunches up on top of you.

Drip. Drip.

It infects you, streaming down your face. You try to breathe, but you can't. Your chest collapses in on itself.

Aaaaaah.

The lights jerk on.

"What's going on?" your roommate shrieks.

You wheeze. "I'm…I'm sorry. I didn't…" You exhale. "It was a nightmare. I'm sorry for waking you up."

You try to smile but you only manage to slightly move your mouth. The shock in your roommate's eyes softens, and he nods toward you.

As soon as he turns off the light, you see the red again. You inhale deeply and close your eyes.

.　　.　　.

Beep. Beep.

The bell on the intercom jerks you awake from your light sleep. You can feel the heavy bags under your eyes.

You roll off your bed and make your way to the bathroom. You slam into someone, an iron hand grabbing your shoulders.

"Watch where you're going," a gruff voice grumbles.

"Sorry," you whisper.

The hands move you toward the back of the line. You rub your eyes trying to stay awake, but every time you do, you see the blood.

You know why you're like this. You've always hated them. You've always hated the Rohingya.

But you've never gone this far.

You used to mock them, insult them when you were younger, but actually hurting them—you've never done that.

You can see the blood on your hands and, for some reason, the color unleashes something in you. You can take your eyes off it.

It's so beautiful.

It's so alluring.

No, no, you shake your head. It's not. Blood is not supposed to be beautiful. It's supposed to be gut-wrenching.

But at the same time, it fills you up. You're finally helping your country. You're finally helping your country by getting rid of the criminals in your country. You're actually doing something.

Your heart flutters as you enter the bathroom.

. . .

"Kan? Come here for a second."

Throughout the day, you've struggled to stay awake. You've caught yourself falling asleep every few minutes. The professor's words pass from one ear to another.

"Is everything alright?" Sayar Nay asks.

You nod, trying to look composed. "Yes, sir. I just didn't get enough sleep last night."

"Make sure to get some rest after classes are over. You don't want to fall back during the start of

your career. If you come back like this again, I'll
have to be stricter with you. Understand?" he says.

"Yes, sir. It won't happen again."

CHAPTER 47

TAREK

AS SOON AS Haya wakes up, we all know it. At the earliest sign of light, a sharp cry goes out and everyone rushes to Mama's room to find Haya screaming and crying.

But after the second day of crying, everyone brushes her cries aside because they know she will only stop with me. The black bags under my eyes grow and every morning, I struggle to stay awake. As soon as Haya falls asleep in my lap, I doze off right there until Grandpa wakes me up.

Every evening is the same routine too. Come back, force Uncle to eat something, sit down with him as he talks and cries and then dinner time, when Haya starts crying again.

I try to live through the day with a smile, but every day, it gets harder and harder.

You've got to keep this up for your family. Do it for them, not for you. They need to have someone who is not breaking down. Someone who can hold them up.

As soon as you're alone in your bed, the smile fades away and you bite away your own tears.

Someone in this family has to be strong or else everything will fall apart.

But even then, sometimes, you let a glass bead drip down your cheek.

.   .   .

Knock. Knock.

I enter Uncle's room and close the door behind me.

I grunt as I sit down, my limbs exhausted from the lack of sleep and overload of work.

"Here, Uncle. Time to eat."

He sits up. Even though he sleeps all day, his eyes are still encompassed by dark shadows and a line runs down both of his cheeks.

"Take it back, Tarek," he mutters before ducking back under the covers.

"Come on, Uncle. We've had the same conversation for the past few days. You *have* to eat," I say. I try to keep my tone gentle, but there's a hint of irritation in it.

Uncle doesn't seem to care. He stays under the covers. I stay silent, trying to keep myself calm.

Creaeeek.

I turn to see Haya peeking through the door, her eyes red. I turn back to Uncle.

"Alright, I'll leave you to eat. I'll be back in a few minutes. Please, *please* eat," I say and get up.

As I leave the room, I massage my tight back and rub my face, trying to wipe away the fatigue. I close the door behind me and kneel down to Haya's eye level.

"Yes?"

She doesn't say anything but pulls herself up to my shoulder with my neck. I stand up and pace around the room, patting her back. Soon, her chest rises and falls rhythmically while her gentle snores ring in my ear. I lay her down in the living room and go back into Uncle's room.

When I enter, he's still under the covers, but the bowl is half-eaten.

"Why don't you finish your food?" I nudge him, holding the bowl near him.

"I don't feel like it," he responds like a child who doesn't want to eat vegetables.

"Please, Uncle," I beg him.

No response.

"You know, Harsa used to be like you. She moved here when the both of us were in our mid-teen years. I was one of the average students in one of the house-schools and the teacher assigned her to help me when I needed it. She would annoy me so much that, just to get her to stop, I would finish my homework. But she continued to nudge me toward better habits. Like you. She was just more annoying than you," he chuckles.

"If that worked back then, I'm pretty sure it'll work now and you'll finish your food too," I respond and Uncle's eyes soften.

He reaches toward the bowl and chews slowly as if thinking about what to say next. But he doesn't say anything. As soon as the last bite is in his mouth, he pulls his blanket back up.

I grab his bowl and leave the room, my heart heavy.

CHAPTER 48

KAN

YOU BARELY MANAGE to keep up with conversation during lunch. Bennu, Cetan and Htun's words pass through your ears. The world is slow, each minuscule movement clear like a movie scene.

Your friends' lips moving.

The other students' footsteps.

It's as if you can see each word hanging in the air.

"Kan? Kan?" A voice pulls you out of your trance.

You turn toward Cetan. All three of them are staring at you. "Hm?" you barely muster.

"Are you okay?"

You nod. "Tired."

Cetan nods cautiously and they go back to their conversation. Occasionally, you catch one of them glancing toward you.

· · ·

As soon as classes are over, you bolt to your room. The thought of your bed makes you want to melt onto the floor.

You force yourself to stay upright. The keyhole keeps moving and you jab at it, frequently hitting the door.

Click.

It finally slides into place and you muster all your strength to turn it. The darkness inside relaxes you even more. You stumble toward the bed, your head hitting the mattress.

But as soon as your eyes close, the red seeps in. It floods in from every direction, pooling into the room. Soon, it lurches toward your dangling ankles and you jerk toward the wall.

You push yourself into the wall as much as possible, trying to keep yourself away.

But the blood inches toward you.

You can hear its cackle, its evil laugh.

"No, no," you scream.

Your eyes jerk open. The red fades away, as if it was never there in the first place.

You sit up straight and inhale deeply, trying to calm your pounding heart.

You lie back down and close your eyes again, and there it is again. You open your eyes and turn toward the wall until your mind cracks open and the black wraps its heavy blanket around you.

CHAPTER 49

TAREK

I WAKE UP to the screaming. I look up at the barely covered window, at the red surge of light flooding in. I dart out of the room toward the crying.

Haya rolls around the living room floor, her face bright red. I scoop her up and rub her back. Her screams get quieter and soon, her inhales turning raspy.

"You didn't come," she whispers. "You didn't come when I was crying."

I swallow. "I-I'm sorry."

She hiccups on a sob. "You didn't hear me."

As soon as she falls asleep, I sit down, still rocking back and forth. Her breathing is a bit labored and from her nose, I can hear where some of the air is blocked. I lay my head against hers and sleep overtakes me.

.   .   .

"How about you come with me today?" I hear in my sleep. I try to force my eyes open, but they refuse to budge.

"It's my break, Grandpa. I haven't gotten one in over two years. Why does Tarek deserve a break instead of me?"

"Ali, look at him. He barely gets any sleep, and he's taking care of Haya and Uncle single-handedly. Everyone's always in their rooms, but he makes sure everyone is taken care of. He wakes up before sunrise for her and then comes with me to work. Don't you think it's fair to give him a day off?"

Ali grumbles. "Fine."

"Let him sleep for one day. He's your brother, after all, and that's what family does for one another."

I can sense the irritation in Ali's limbs. I want to get up and say that I can go, but I can't. I can't move, I can't open my eyes, I can't speak.

Before I can muster any energy, the back door *creaks* closed and my brain shuts down again.

.   .   .

My eyes flutter open when Haya starts squirming. Her eyes are shut tightly, but she struggles to move. I pat her back and rub it, trying to make the nightmare go away.

It doesn't work.

She begins to kick and punch. She opens her mouth and I cover my ears.

A sharp shriek echoes through the house. I get up and walk around, patting her back, but it's no use. Soon, her eyes crack open, but her wails continue.

"It's okay. It's okay," I whisper into her ear.

She buries her face into my shirt. "I'm hungry," she says, her voice muffled.

I walk into the kitchen and set her on the counter. She watches me with heavy, dark eyes as I crack an egg on the pan. A few minutes later, I set her down on the dinner cloth and she picks at her food.

"I don't want to eat," she mutters.

"Didn't you say you were hungry?"

"Not anymore." Haya pushes the plate away from her.

"You have to eat or else you won't grow. Do you want to stay tiny? Then, I'll be able to tickle you every day and you won't be able to do anything."

A slight smile tugs at her lips. "Are you going to eat?"

"I have to make my food first. Start eating and I'll be down here before you finish."

She nods and cautiously puts a bite into her mouth. Her stomach shrieks and she eats another bite. I crack another egg, watching as it turns from a liquid into a solid.

A minute later, I'm sitting down next to Haya, both of us gobbling our food. I watch as she puts bite after bite into her mouth. Soon, her eyes are locked on my plate.

"Can I have more?" she whispers.

I put down my food. "What's the magic word?"

"Please?" she asks, showing all of her tiny teeth.

I nod and hand her my plate.

"Here, I'm full. How about you finish this for me?" I say. My stomach aches for more.

Haya looks up at me and nods enthusiastically. As soon as she finishes, I put both plates in the sink, waiting for Haya to leave the kitchen. As soon as she disappears behind the door, I grab two figs and toss them into my mouth.

CHAPTER 50

KAN

"AS NEW SOLDIERS, you all will have the opportunity to get a city duty. This will allow you to be prepared for future jobs you will have. However, not everyone will get accepted, so please try your best on the application. You will receive the sign-up form in your emails later on. Class is dismissed," Sayar Zaw announces as soon as the clock strikes twelve for lunch.

The buzz of excited students rings through the hall.

"City duty."

"Sounds fun."

"It'll be like a job."

Bennu bumps into me. "Are you thinking of doing the duty?" he asks.

"Of course. I might as well try to get accepted. You?" you respond.

"You'll get into it for sure. You're every teacher's favorite. If they don't accept you, no one is going to get in. I want to try too. It sounds like a good opportunity to get out. I'm kind of tired of the exact same schedule every single day," he says.

You nod. The blandness of it gets to you. It makes you see the red more often.

You shudder, thinking about the nightmares, about the blood seeping on to you.

"Hurry up. Cetan and Htun must be waiting for us," Bennu scurries forward, weaving through the crowd. You struggle to keep up with him.

Bennu glances over his shoulder a couple of times, beckoning you to pick up the pace.

You feel the vibration of a phone in your pocket. It's probably the email. Your heart jumps.

.   .   .

"Alright, before you all go for lunch, check the posters on the wall. Why, you may ask? It has your duty results."

At the sound of "duty," a burst of chatter explodes. Everyone runs down the stairs and out the door.

Bennu jumps up and down with excitement. "Come on already. Why are you taking so long to pack your things? Don't you want to see if you got in?"

You chuckle. "I am, I am but everyone is already there and it'll be too crowded. We should wait so it'll be easier to see our names."

"Oooo, you're right. That's why you're the genius of the group," Bennu exclaims.

You scoff. "Yeah, right. Half of the students here are smarter than me. I'm not the genius."

"I never said the genius of the school. I said, the genius of the group."

You turn red. "Oh."

"Everyone's gone now. Let's go."

.   .   .

A few seconds later, you stare at your name printed on the paper.

Rejected, it says printed in red.

Your heart drops and you resist the urge to grip your pounding head.

You gulp and glance over to Bennu's name. He moves toward you, reading over your shoulder. His smile falls once he sees the red next to your name.

"I'm sorry, Kan. You'll be accepted next time. I know it."

"What about you?" you ask.

He frowns. "Maybe next time."

Your happiness fades away. "I'm so—"

"You should have seen your face!" Bennu shrieks. "I got in. But...I won't be able to spend as much time with you."

You shrug your shoulders, but inside, your heart is squirming. You were good enough. You're not as successful as you thought you would be. You *failed.*

Bennu puts his hand on your shoulder. "Don't beat yourself over it, Kan. In life, there are speed bumps that cause us to jump into the air. In that moment, we forget all the success behind us and all we see is a crash landing. But at some point, we'll settle onto the ground and keep moving forward. That's what matters."

You smile, but the disappointment still spreads throughout you.

CHAPTER 51

TAREK

FOR THE FIRST time, Haya doesn't wake up screaming. She doesn't wake up crying. She slept in peacefully, smiling in her sleep.

And for the first time, I also slept peacefully as if I've never experienced sleep before. No one bothered to wake me up.

But in my dreams, Uncle opened his door for the first time, his hair combed back and wearing clean clothes. In my dreams, he walked with a smile and accompanied Grandpa outside.

· · ·

I wake up, sweat dripping down my face. I rub my eyes, trying to get used to the light.

The light?

I jump out of bed and run into the living room. "Where's Grandpa? Where's Grandpa?" I exclaim.

Grandma peers out of her room. "Gone for work. Why?"

"I was supposed to go with him," I wheeze, my mind spinning. He went by himself. I should have woken up earlier. Now he has to work by himself.

Grandma smiles at me. "Yusuf went with him."

I jerk and turn toward her. "What?" I gawk.

"Your uncle went with him. He got ready and came out of his room when your Grandpa was about to leave."

"He did?"

She nods.

I shrug my shoulders. People are quite odd sometimes. One moment they're crying their eyes and the next moment, they're laughing and jumping.

Crreeeeak.

The door to Mama's room cracks open and Haya peeks her head outside. Her face lights up when she sees me.

"Tarek!" she shrieks and charges toward me, jumping up. I catch her and she hugs me.

Humans really are interesting. What happened? Everyone is slightly normal now. But whatever it is, I don't want it to fade away.

"Let's play," she says.

I laugh. "I haven't even brushed my teeth yet. I first have to change and eat breakfast. Then I have to study and then we'll play."

She pouts. "Can you do those things fast?"

I chuckle. "I'll try."

"Okay."

"I mean it. I'll try my best."

Haya jumps off me. "I'm going to play with my dolls in that time."

I watch as she disappears into Mama's room, smiling for the first time in a while.

. . .

I clean the kitchen right after breakfast, humming as I wash the dishes. As soon as I dry my hands on the towels, I go to the living room and pull out some books.

I finish right before Grandpa and Uncle open the door. As soon as I hear the door slide open, I jump up.

My dream was...real? Uncle's smiling for the first time and his hair is combed. He's changed his clothes after wearing the same ones for two weeks.

"Uncle?" I whisper.

He wraps me in a bear hug. "Thank you for everything."

I rub his back and a spot of water spreads on my shoulder. Uncle pulls away and peers into my eyes. "Thank you. Thank you."

I force the heaviness in my eyes away. "You don't need to thank me. I'm your nephew and we're a family. If we, if I, don't take care of you, who will?"

He kisses the top of my head and wipes the beads in his eyes. He turns to Mama. "You've raised him well."

Mama smiles and her eyes glitter. "We all have," she whispers.

"Who wants to play a game of soccer?"

.   .   .

A few hours later, we all barrel into the house, our clothes stuck to our bodies. Haya giggles as Mama takes her to the bathroom to take a shower. Everyone else takes turns in the bathrooms.

Grandma heads to the kitchen, the *click* of the stoves reaching my ears.

Something blue blinds me. I peel the towel away and blink at the thrower.

"Wipe yourself off while we wait for the shower." Uncle chuckles, but I can still see a hint of sadness lingering in his eyes. It's as if they're half brown and half blue.

I smile back at him and rub the towel around my neck. My skin is still sticky, but it works.

CHAPTER 52

KAN

YOU PACE AROUND your room, a book in your hands. Now that you're even busier than ever, you need to be as efficient as possible. You need to make sure you don't fall behind.

Bzzz. Bzzz. Bzz.

Your phone vibrates. After you finish the page, you whip it out.

Bennu: How about we eat out tonight? I'm bored.

Htun: I'm up for it.

Bennu: Of course you would say yes to food. What about you, Kan and Cetan?

You type out a response and send it without a care.

Kan: Sure.

You crave anything but the normal food. Instantly, your mother's face appears. Your mouth waters at the thought of her cooking.

Focus. Focus. You've got to focus on your job. Don't think about food right now.

You shake your head and put your head back into your book.

.   .   .

"Everyone done?" Cetan asks, searching everyone's empty plates.

You nod and Htun muffles his belch. "Alright, I'll pay." Bennu slides some cash but you snatch the bill from him, taking half of it out and replacing it with your own cash.

Within a split second, Bennu is leaning over you, trying to reach for the bill. You keep it away from him.

"I'm paying half," you assert.

"No, I want to. Come on. Please," he asks, but you keep the bill away.

You beckon a waiter over and hand the bill to him. Bennu collapses into his chair, pouting. You grin and he punches your arm.

"I'll be prepared next time," he whines.

"Let's head back. We could take a long walk," Htun says, pushing back his chair. You all follow him out of the restaurant. Soon, the lights are behind you and you're in the same dark street you were in last time.

You blink as you watch red seep in from the alleys. You shake your head, trying to shove the image out, but it flows toward you, licking your ankles.

You hold your flinch and search ahead. A man carrying a sack over his shoulder walks in the opposite direction. You glance toward the group. All of them have their eyes glued to him.

"That Rohingya doesn't deserve to walk these streets," Bennu whispers in your ear.

You straighten at the sound of the hatred in his voice. But something inside you smiles, warming you up. Bennu nods to Cetan and Htun and they cut the man off.

You drink the terror in his eyes.

"Looks like we found ourselves a dirty man," Cetan says, pushing the man down. He crumples like paper and his lip quivers.

"Please—" he whispers, but before he can move, a river of red flows out from his stomach. His eyes widen and then the life floats out of them. He falls back with a *thud* onto the dirt.

You watch with a grin on your face, savoring the red.

CHAPTER 53

TAREK

BY THE TIME everyone is done showering, the sun is barely peeking over the horizon. The wafting smell of fish and rice travels through the air, lighting a fire in my stomach.

Haya and Grandpa are already sitting on the floor. Both of them are having some sort of competition for who can make the goofiest face.

"Now we have two toddlers in the house," Grandma chuckles as she sits down next to Grandpa.

I peel my eyes off the steaming fish and my stomach growls.

"You can eat if you want to," Grandma says.

"I'll wait for everyone else," I respond.

A minute later, all of us are digging into the fish, the warmth sliding down my throat.

"It's delicious, Grandma," I say after I swallow the first bite.

She grins at me.

"When has your grandmother *not* made delicious food?" Grandpa asks.

"Don't listen to him," Grandma says, still beaming.

"He's right though," Mama remarks and laughs when Grandma shoots her a playful don't you dare look.

For the first time, it's a little normal. A little like how it was before.

"Ali, you seem awfully quiet," Uncle says. Ali shrugs his shoulders.

"I've been meaning to say something," he mutters.

"Go ahead," Grandma says.

"I've been thinking of joining an organization," he says.

Grandpa's eyes light up. "Are you considering the mosque's organization? You're going to volunteer?"

Everyone turns with bright eyes. Ali swallows hard, but no one seems to notice. No one but me.

Something tugs at my stomach.

"Actually, it's more like a...political organization."

Everyone freezes, the light in their eyes quickly shadowed.

"What do you mean political organization?" Mama asks. I can hear her heart pounding from across her.

"It's called ARSA and—"

"Stop," Grandpa interrupts, "You want to join ARSA? Are you insane?"

Red flashes over Ali's face. "I'm a grown man. I can decide what I want to do."

"What?" Mama turns toward Grandpa, her face pale. "What's ARSA?"

Grandpa grits your teeth and swallows. "They are an organization centered on bringing glory back to the Rohingya people. They are terrorists—"

"They are not," Ali growls. "You don't know anything about them. How do you know they're a terrorist group? Through the rumors going around town?"

"They resort to murder. They kill people," Grandpa responds. "This is not Islam. This is not what glory is. If this is what it takes to bring us back to normalcy, I would rather live in oppression."

"That's *you*," Ali shrieks, "I don't want to live like this anymore. Their message makes sense. If the government doesn't give us respect, we need to take it."

I glance toward Mama. Her normally reddish face is now ghostly. Grandpa turns to her.

"There's another thing you need to know, Asma." He glances toward Uncle and Uncle's face freezes. He shakes his head but Grandpa ignores him. "These people, ARSA, the government thought that Saleh was a part of them. That's why they...targeted him."

There's a split second of agonizing silence.

"No one bothered to tell me this," Mama whispers. "No one thought I deserved to know this. He was *my* husband, and you all hid this from me."

"It was to protect you," Grandma says.

"So that the truth would suddenly be dropped onto me? And you," she turns to Ali, "how dare you speak about them like that? How can you speak so kindly about the reason your father's dead?"

"Asma—" Grandpa tries to say, but she cuts him off.

"No, it's my turn to speak now."

I tug on her sleeve. "What about Haya?"

"Go to the room," she tells Haya and Haya scurries out of the kitchen.

Mama turns back to Ali. "You may be an adult but you're still part of a family. The decisions you make, the decisions we all make, impact each and every person in this house. Don't you dare make selfish decisions."

Ali's face is bright red and I can see him biting his tongue. We came up with that solution a long time ago. If one of us got angry, that person would bite their tongue from saying anything they would regret.

But that doesn't mean anger can't take control of our actions. Ali pushes away from the dinner cloth and storms out of the kitchen.

Thump. Thump. Slam.

Our room's door slams shut, shaking the house.

CHAPTER 54

KAN

YOU GO BACK to your dorm. Something inside you snapped. Something enlivening, something warm. You savor a rush of energy in your limbs and even though it's dark outside, you feel as if you just woke up.

You should be drained. You took the life of a person. You committed murder.

You shake the thought away. That man didn't deserve to walk. He wasn't a person. He didn't deserve to live. You're doing a favor to your country. Isn't that why you're in the Tatmadaw?

Besides, if killing was such a bad thing, you wouldn't feel so refreshed, you wouldn't feel so exhilarated. Bad things are supposed to make you feel guilty but you've never been better.

Bzzzz. Bzzzzzz.

Your phone vibrates constantly and you pull yourself out of your thoughts. You pull your phone out and stare at the tag on the screen.

Mama.

You answer it and place the phone on your ear.

"Kan!" Your mother screams with joy. "It's been a while since you last called so I thought I would call."

"I'm busy," you spit. You immediately regret it but you keep the same annoyed face on. You don't bother apologizing.

You can hear her shock. "I-I'm sorry. I know but you must have a few minutes sometimes, right?"

"I'm studying all day."

You try to stop yourself but the poison from your mouth never ends.

"Alright. How are you doing?"

"Fine."

Silence. You want to ask her how she's doing but something keeps your mouth shut.

"Have you made friends?" she whispers.

"Yeah."

"How is everything else?"

"Fine. It's fine. Everything is fine."

"Are you sure?" she asks, her breath shaking.

"Yes."

"You don't sound fine. You're different, Kan. I'm concerned. Maybe this wasn't such a good idea. Maybe you should come home."

"This is my home. I'm an adult now, Mama. I can think for myself. I can go where I want to. I'm not going back home just so you have someone to keep you company."

She inhales sharply. You've crossed a line. "Alright. I apologize for calling you. I apologize for interrupting your busy schedule. Let me know when you're available and then I'll call," she whispers.

The call hangs up.

Guilt tugs at your heart but you shake it away. You have much more important things to do than talk on the phone.

You spy Bennu coming from the hall. He waves and notices your sullen expression.

"Having trouble dealing with the incident?" he asks once he nears you.

You shrug.

"Don't worry. It gets easier."

"With what? Time?" You ask.

"No, it gets easier the more you do it."

CHAPTER 55

TAREK

TAP. TAP.

I knock on our room's door. The faint sound of a blanket rustling floats through the wood.

Creeaak.

"I'm coming in," I announce.

No response.

I throw open the door but the lump under the blanket doesn't move. He doesn't acknowledge that I'm here. He doesn't tell me to get out of the room.

He's just silent.

And that's what scares me the most.

I can feel the heat radiating from him as I cross over to my mat. I tug my blanket up my legs but leave my arms out. I stare at the lump.

"Are you alright?" I whisper.

Ali shifts but doesn't respond.

"I know you heard me," I prompt.

The heat intensifies.

"Why are you ignoring me?"

The lump shoots up like a blur. "Don't. Talk. To. Me," Ali says with gritted teeth.

"Why?"

"Because you're a coward. All of you are cowards. You all want a *peaceful* life but you don't fight for yourselves. You tolerate all of this oppression because you're afraid. I don't deserve to live here among cowards."

A needle of hurt pricks my heart. "We're trying to look out for our family. ARSA is dangerous. Someone will get hurt. What will happen to Mama if she finds out the government is after you?"

He collapses back into his mat, not a single word said in response. I open my mouth to say something but nothing comes out. When Ali is angry, nothing can cool him down. Nothing except for time.

I lie down and turn away from him, the darkness creeping from the corners.

.   .   .

My leg jerks, waking me up. I roll out of my crumpled blanket and slap my face, trying to wipe the sleepiness from my face. The blurs around the room grow crisp.

My eyes land on the mat next to me. The blanket is thrown off to the side.

I shrug. I guess Ali wanted to wake up early. I gently crack open the door and enter the bathroom. I turn toward the cup with all of our toothbrushes.

As a habit, I count all of them.

One.

Two.

Three.

Four.

Five.

Six.

I shake my head and count again.

One.

Two.

Three.

Four.

Five.

Six.

There are supposed to be seven. I search through them and my heart drops. Ali's is missing.

Maybe he dropped it somewhere or misplaced it. Nothing to worry about. You're overthinking.

I brush my teeth and throw on a pair of clothes. I enter the kitchen.

"Ali?" I ask, peering into the room.

No one.

I go to the back, peering into the stall. The cart's still there so Ali can't be with Grandpa.

So where is he?

I search the entire house, finding his clothes and shoes missing. I grip the back of my neck and try to slow my racing heart.

There has to be a logical explanation. He couldn't have just vanished...right?

But something tugs at my stomach. Another door *creaks* open. I spin around, hoping to see Ali but instead, I'm greeted by Grandpa.

His smile fades away. "Is everything alright?" he whispers.

"Where's Ali?" I wheeze, my mouth sandy.

He shrugs. "I just woke up so I wouldn't know. Have you checked around the house?"

I nod.

"He could have gone to the market to buy something. Maybe we're out of eggs or something. Check."

Both of us bolt into the kitchen and throw open the fridge. Everything we need is right there.

"We're not missing anything," I croak.

"Alright. Stay here. I'll go to the market and check around town."

Grandpa grabs his hat and before a word is said, the back door slams shut.

CHAPTER 56

KAN

YOU MAKE A bee-line toward the table after grabbing lunch. You place your plate next to Bennu, your stomach gurgling at the sight of the fish, rice and steamed vegetables.

"Any news?" Htun asks everyone.

You shrug. Nothing interesting has happened.

"No, just classes, work and homework," Cetan says.

"I know right? Life's been too monotonous these days. The interesting things only happen when we're out and about. It's the same schedule day after day," Bennu elaborates.

"We should go out next week after our tests. I need to practice for my shooting exam. I want to get as close to the bull's eye as possible," Cetan says.

"Yeah, and next time." Htun's eyes dart to me. He leans in to whisper and Bennu and Cetan turn their ears toward us. "*You* should be the one to plunge the knife into the next victim's body."

You swallow the small lump in your throat. It's one thing to enjoy watching the blood but causing it makes your stomach churn.

"What? Are you afraid of a little blood?" Htun teases but you know that he doesn't mean to hurt you.

"It's just that...it's just that I've never you know." You run your fingers along your neck in a sharp, quick motion.

"So?" Cetan interjects. "There's always a first time. Me and Bennu had our first one when we were at home and we caught a girl stealing food from our trash. Imagine! Trash having the audacity to steal *our* food." Bennu scoffs when Cetan ends his story.

"My first one was the boy in the alley," Htun says. It certainly didn't seem like it was his first time. Maybe he's just naturally good at this?

"The point is," Cetan says, "You have to try. Htun's right. Next time, you'll do the honors."

A sly smile spreads on his face and you can't help the smirk growing in yours. You nod, imagining the blood seeping between his fingers.

CHAPTER 57

TAREK

I PACE IN front of the back door, anticipation biting at my heart. The food in my stomach threatens to climb out.

After an eternity, the door knob turns and a straw hat pokes from behind the door. Grandpa's serious face is all I need to know.

He shakes his head and my heartbeat speeds up. The tight, sullen expression glued to his face makes my blood run cold.

"He's...gone, right? He ran away, didn't he?" I mutter.

Grandpa grunts and nods.

My heart sinks.

Ali ran away. He ran away to join ARSA. He ran away and put his family in danger.

"Don't say a word about this to anyone. I'll be the one to tell them," Grandpa huffs and puts his face in his hands.

I sit down next to him, wrapping an arm around his shoulder. He turns toward me. All of a sudden, he looks older. The wrinkles on his face, the white hair, the trembling hands. I can see it all.

His eyes water and I tighten my arm against him. We sit in silence, Grandpa staring blankly at the wall.

A few moments later, he trudges to the kitchen and clicks the stove on. I sink into the cushions.

Our family is falling apart. First Aunt Harsa and now Ali. It's as if a piece of my heart has been ripped out. We only had each other in this mess but even that is slowly crumbling.

I close my eyes but every time I do, the silence rings in my ear. The icy, deep silence of a house. Of a home that used to protect a happy family. A home that used to protect laughter and joy. But now, it only holds sorrow and pain.

I turn my head slightly as I hear noise behind everyone else's doors. I grab my books and shut my room's door behind me, trying to guard my heaviness.

A pained cry echoes from the living room. I place my pencil in my notebook and peek through a crack in the door.

Fat, glistening tears splat onto the floor. Mama's hand covers her mouth and a few strands of hair stick to her wet face. Grandma guides Mama to the floor cushions and Grandma and Grandpa sit on either side of her, rubbing her back and stroking her hair.

A knife twists in my heart. Uncle appears from the kitchen and sits on the floor in front of Mama. He doesn't move. He doesn't say anything. He just looks at her with soft, understanding eyes.

"My own son left me," she cries. "He left me."

No one says anything.

"I love him so, so much and he left me, his own mother."

I swallow the lump in my throat and retreat deeper into the shadows, wrapping myself in my blanket.

.   .   .

The next morning, Mama doesn't leave her room. Not to eat, not to go to the bathroom.

I knock on her door but not a single sound responds. I open the door to find Mama in her bed, her breathing heavy.

"Mama?" I whisper.

"Hm?" she wheezes.

"What do you want to eat?" I ask her.

She cracks open her eyes. "Nothing."

"You have to eat something."

"I'll throw up if I eat anything."

As my eyes adjust to the darkness, I spot the splotches of red on her face. I place my hand against her forehead and immediately pull it back.

"I'll be right back," I tell her, trying to hide the panic from my voice.

I close the door a little bit and go to the kitchen. "Grandma?" I ask.

She turns toward me. "Yes?"

"Mama's sick."

Her soft expression morphs to panic. "What?"

"Mama's sick."

"Are you sure?" she asks.

I nod. "Her forehead is burning."

"Alright, I'll take care of her." Grandma smiles at me. "Don't worry. Continue on with your day. You're not going to university if you don't study."

I smile back at her. But I can't tell her that I've changed my mind. I would have gone if Aunt and Ali were here but now, I can't leave. It'll be difficult for everyone. I don't want to cause any difficulty.

CHAPTER 58

KAN

"DID YOU HEAR about ARSA?"

"Did you hear about the attacks?"

"ARSA."

"ARSA."

"ARSA."

All day, that's all you hear. Everyone you meet asks you about the attacks. Yes, you know about them. You know about the ARSA attacks in Maung-Dau.

"Alright, everyone, settle down now," Sayar Nay exclaims when he enters the classroom. The entire room is buzzing with conversation, students excited about the new developments in the Rakhine State.

"Class time," Sayar Nay says again, impatiently. The room dials down to a hush.

He nods, satisfied, "Now, I know you all are talking about the attacks in Maung-Dau. I have been informed that the commanders have decided to dispatch the Tatmadaw over there to ensure there is no more chaos. Most of you will also be dispatched with them. You will hear an announcement in the evening and you will leave tomorrow morning. As for the remainder who aren't doing well in their studies, you will remain on campus and will have a study hall for the days everyone is out. Is that clear?"

You examine the room, sensing a mix of emotion in the air. Some people are happy they get to leave and experience a change of scenery. Others are irritated that they'll have to stay on campus while some of their friends go on adventures.

You glance at Bennu, who is jittery with excitement. "We get to be *real* soldiers, Kan," he whisper-yells in your ear.

You smile. "I know. I can't wait."

"The rest of the day is going to pass by *so* slowly now. I wish they would have surprised us instead," Bennu pouts.

Sayar Nay clears his throat and the whispering ceases immediately. "Just because other things are happening doesn't mean there's no class."

"Who's excited for our field trip?" Bennu announces when he arrives at the lunch table.

Cetan and Htun blink. "Htun's not going," Cetan says.

Bennu's expression changes. "Oh... Sorry."

Htun picks at his food. "I really wanted to go. It would have been a real-life experience as a soldier. I want to be an actual soldier already."

"One day, we'll all be in the army and we'll never have to study again. It'll be all action. We just have to wait," you say, still staring at your food.

CHAPTER 59

TAREK

I CRACK OPEN the door to retrieve today's newspaper.

ARSA Attacks a Maung-Dau Police Station.

I blink and read the headline again.

ARSA Attacks a Maung-Dau Police Station.

My stomach threatens to climb up to my throat and my heart beats in my ears. Ali was with them. Ali is among those who attacked the station.

I sit down, putting the newspaper beside me. I try to calm my heartbeat down but it gets faster and faster.

ThumpThump.

ThumpThump.

ThumpThump.

Grandpa comes out from the bathroom. "Everything alright, Tarek?" he asks.

I hand the newspaper to him. He scans the headline and his eyes widen. He blinks at me with shocked, fearful eyes.

"This...this is going to be the end," he mutters.

My throat goes dry. "Wha—what do you mean?"

"The government will imprison Ali for being a part of this. He'll die in there." Tears rim the edge of Grandpa's eyes.

The thought of a dark, damp cell appears. Chains hang from the wall while a bucket resides in the corner.

I cover my mouth and dash toward the bathroom. I inhale slowly after I vomit, standing over the toilet in case I need to throw up again.

"Your mother can't find out about this. It'll kill her."

My heart sinks. "But it'll kill her if we *don't* tell her," I whisper.

"She's fragile right now. She can't deal with the burden of more bad news. We'll tell her when she's stronger."

I want to protest but the thought of Mama collapsing onto the floor sends a blizzard through my veins.

"Don't mention this to anyone, alright? It's best that this stays between the two of us," Grandpa says. He doesn't even need to turn around to check if I agree. Because he knows I do.

.   .   .

"What's ARSA?" Haya asks at dinner time.

Me and Grandpa stop chewing and glance at each other before turning toward Haya.

"Where did you hear that from?" I ask, trying to remain as normal as possible. Mama glares at me as if she can see the invisible pool of sweat, as if she can see how I'm drowning in my nervousness.

"Some of the kids were talking about it. They said that someone named ARSA attacked the police," Haya says as if this is the world's most normal news.

"That's just children's talk. You know how people twist things into dramatic stories," Grandpa says, calmly.

I see a hint of doubt in Mama's eyes. "But kids don't always do that," Mama responds.

"They do. They're masters of drama."

"Can I have more?" Haya interrupts the tension in the room.

I hand her my plate. "Here you go, fish monster."

She chuckles. "I need to eat to grow big and strong. See." She stands up and when she does, she barely reaches my head.

"I'll be bigger than you one day," she pouts and sits back down.

I smile. "I know you will."

.	.	.

"Come on, time to go to bed," I announce and lift Haya off the ground.

"Can I play for five more minutes? Please?"

"If you want to become big and strong, you need to sleep on time. No staying up late, alright? You've been playing for hours and your body needs rest," I respond and take her to the bathroom.

I help her brush her teeth and wash her face. A few minutes later, I'm tucking her into her mat, wrapping her in her blanket like a mummy.

"Good night, Tarek," Haya whispers.

"Good night, Haya," I respond, closing the door behind me.

CHAPTER 60

KAN

"SEE YOU TOMORROW," Bennu shouts as he continues walking down the hall. Cetan pouts next to him.

"Do you have to keep mentioning this again and again to everyone, especially Htun?" he whines.

"You can't blame me. I'm excited," Bennu counters.

I smile and wave right before they turn left and disappear. The door opens and you step into the cool room. The curtains are pulled back, revealing the landscape outside.

You place your bag on your bed and lean against the window, watching the sun barely peek above the line of trees. It's a huge ball of red in the middle of the creeping darkness.

It reminds you of the flowing blood.

You smile at the thought of the boy and the man. The sound as the knife slid into their bodies echoes near you, sending a thrill of adrenaline through your veins.

You focus on the sunset outside, your mind wandering to the future. You wonder what it's like to serve in the army. So far, it's been training and hypotheticals.

If the enemy does this, then do this.

If you're stranded, then do this.

If you're in close combat with an armed soldier, do this.

And so on.

But other than your imagination, you have no idea what fighting is actually like.

And this will be your first taste of combat, of proving yourself.

You peel your eyes off the sunset and lay down on the bed, staring at the ceiling.

Your excitement can barely be contained. You glance toward your stuff in the closet and sigh. There's no use in packing everything. You'll be back within a day or two. Phones and other things are prohibited. They're already going to give you a lot of heavy equipment.

You get up and pull the curtains, blocking the light. The room is now an inviting black. You

change your clothes and lay down, waiting for the
night to pass.

CHAPTER 61

TAREK

I RUB MY face and open the front door, brushing my hand against the dirt.

Nothing.

I blink a few times and the ground grows crisp. There's nothing in front of the door. There's no newspaper today.

My stomach sinks. There's always a newspaper.

Always.

Maybe they're late. Maybe someone else picked up the paper.

But deep down, I know that something's not right. Something's going on and they don't want us to know.

I try to force the thought out of my mind, but it lingers on the edge, threatening to pour into the black hole at any time.

Something pulls me and a pair of arms wrap around my knees. I jerk before noticing the tiny hands clasped around my knees.

"You're up early," I remark.

"I was too excited," Haya responds.

"For what?"

"I don't know. I'm excited for something."

"I have to move now. Can you let go of me, please?" I ask.

"No," she shrieks and holds on tighter.

I turn in so that I'm facing her and in one quick movement, she's up in the air, screaming with delight.

"Shhhh, everyone's sleeping," I say, gently covering her mouth.

I walk to the kitchen and put Haya onto the counter, cracking two eggs in the pan.

.   .   .

Mama goes to market with Grandma.

"It'll be good for you. You can't stay in the house forever. Let's go enjoy," Grandma says, ignoring Mama's empty eyes.

"It's alright. I want to stay home," Mama responds, inching toward the door.

"No." Grandma grabs her arm and pulls her gently toward the front door. "We're going out. You can't tell me that you don't want to. I'm your mother and you have to listen to me."

Mama sighs, defeated. Grandma places a hat over her head and opens the front door.

"We'll be back in about an hour. Is that alright, Tarek?" she asks.

I nod, smiling from the inside.

The house is empty except for Haya's occasional squeal. It doesn't feel like home anymore. The ghost of memory lingers around the place. The ghosts of Aunt and Ali.

I lay on the dining mat, staring up at the empty ceiling. The clock ticks by, marking each agonizing second.

Click.

The back door swings open and the heavy voices of Uncle and Grandpa echo through the hall.

"Tarek?" Uncle says, stopping dead in his tracks.

I barely lift my head up.

"What are you doing?" he asks, his eyebrows scrunched up.

"I don't know," I respond.

"Where's everyone else?"

"Mama and Grandma went to the market and Haya is outside, playing with the other kids."

"Are you sure Mama and Grandma went? We would have seen them if they were in the market," he asks.

I nod. "They took their hats, and they probably took the long route. Grandma is trying to cheer Mama up," I say.

"Is everything alright with you?" Uncle says, sitting near my head.

I sit up. "Yeah, I'm just tired."

Uncle looks at me with concern, as if he knows that my heart is ripping apart.

"He'll come back. You know that, right?" he whispers.

I shake my head. "He won't."

"He will. He's still young, and he acted impulsively. He'll eventually regret his decision and come back. You're worrying for no reason."

"Alright," I reply but inside, I know my brother. I know that he's afraid of being wrong, that he'd rather suffer than admit that he's wrong. And when he's committed to something, he'll follow through, no matter what.

Uncle gets up to leave. "I know you don't believe me now, but when he walks through that door in a few days, you will."

I want to believe him. I really do, but deep down, I know that Uncle's wrong. I know that Ali isn't going to come home.

PART II:

DURING

CHAPTER 62

KAN

THEY PACK ALL of you into trucks, not a single inch of space between you all. It's dark, the heaviness forming a thick layer of sweat over your skin. You wipe your forehead and listen to the sound of breathing.

Everyone is silent, and it causes a lump to form in your throat. Your stomach sinks as the nervousness tickles your skin. You interlace your fingers and squeeze, trying to get the anxiety to fade away.

You exhale and touch your pocket. You go back to the message you sent to Mama.

Kan: I won't be able to text or call for a while. Going out on duty. Phones aren't allowed.

You didn't get a response when you were there. You can imagine her staring at the message, tears threatening to break out of her eyes.

She won't reply until she realizes that her son isn't a child anymore.

You glance toward Bennu, trying to get a read on his face. But the only thing you can see are the white of his eyes and the silhouette of his face. He turns toward you.

"Everything good?" he whispers.

You nod but realize he can't see you. "Yeah, yeah."

He turns back to staring at the wall. You shift, trying to get your nerves to calm down.

This is the opportunity you've been waiting for. You've been dreaming about going out and fighting. You've been training for this since you were ten. Ever since you knew you were going to become a soldier.

But that was also when the nervousness awakened. That was when the worrying bled into your life. You were worried you weren't able to be strong. You were worried you wouldn't get into the army. You were worried you wouldn't be able to pass the physical examination.

And now, all you want is for that nervousness to go away. You want to be free from its icy grip.

You divert your thoughts to the past few months of training. You've come far. You've made friends and you've persevered in your training.

You see a flash from the corner of your eye. You turn slightly, making sure no one else notices. A flash of red floods in from the corner. You relish its sight. It satisfies something within your heart. It warms you up and relaxes you. You let yourself loose as the anxiety fades away.

You see the toddler and the man drowning in a pool of blood, stab wounds splotched over them. You smile as the sight of Rohingya men, women and children fold onto the floor, the red pooling around your ankles.

CHAPTER 63

TAREK

WHEN MAMA AND Grandma come back home, the fear in their eyes is all I can see. Their faces shine with sweat, their noses slightly flared up. A few bags of food hang from their arms. I reach out to take them.

"Salam Alaikum," Grandpa says and hugs Mama and Grandma.

Mama tries to cover the coldness in her eyes, but it doesn't work. "What's wrong?" Grandpa asks her.

"You didn't tell me about the attacks," Mama whispers.

Grandpa's face turns into a ghostly pale. "I—"

"You were trying to protect me, I know. But it backfired. I found out from strangers. That hurts more."

"Asma, we just thought you were under a lot of stress already and we didn't want to overburden you," Grandpa says.

"We? Who's the other person?"

Grandpa's eyes dart to me and Mama's eyes widen. "Tarek? Tarek knew about this too?"

I want to melt into the floor.

Tears flood into Mama's eyes and she peels her eyes off me. "You tried to hide news about my son when I am his *mother?*" Her voice cracks. "You tried to hide my son's crimes from *me?*"

"We tried to protect you," Grandma says, putting her hand around Mama's shoulder.

"Protecting me by hiding the truth? What if Ali had died? Would you have kept it from me to protect me? Doesn't a mother deserve to know about her child?"

"It's not like that—" Grandpa says.

"It's exactly like that," Mama interrupts. "It's *exactly* like that."

Mama slips her shoes off and slams the door of her room. Grandma smiles sadly at Grandpa.

"You should have told her. You should have at least told me," she whispers and goes into her room.

My feet are glued to the floor while a lump sinks in my throat. Grandpa retreats to his room, leaving me alone in the middle of the living room.

.   .   .

"Why is everyone so quiet?" Haya asks as everyone stares at the food in front of us.

Uncle smiles at her. "We're just tired." He reaches out to get a few plates and cuts the fish into equal pieces. He hands the plates to Grandpa, Grandma and Mama.

He gestures for me to take some and I do, putting some on Haya's plate. She digs into her food as I eat carefully, monitoring everyone.

Mama just stares at her plate blankly. Uncle nudges her and she looks up at him.

"You have to eat," he whispers, but she doesn't move.

He sets his spoon down. "I won't eat until you do."

Mama glares at him but she still doesn't touch her plate. Uncle leans against the wall, interlacing his fingers. Mama just stares. First at her food and then at Uncle.

The minutes slow down, a blanket of heaviness descending onto us. Mama inches toward her spoon and puts a morsel of food in her mouth. Uncle smiles and eats a morsel as well.

Mama blinks and sighs, eating a bigger bite this time. Uncle copies her, and this continues until both of their plates are wiped clean.

I glance toward Haya beside me and she stares, her eyebrows scrunched up. She hops to Mama and hugs her. "What's wrong?"

"Everything's fine," she responds. "What's wrong is that it's past your bedtime. Tarek, do you mind helping her?"

I get up and step out of the kitchen, watching as Haya follows. The tension in Mama's voice sends chills down my spine.

"Alright. Hurry up," I tell Haya, and she runs to change her clothes. I help her with brushing and washing her face, all while focused on the kitchen. Not a single sound comes from there.

As soon as I open the door to Mama's room, a hushed voice speaks in the kitchen. I rush to put Haya down to bed.

"Hug?" she asks as I'm about to leave. Her arms are outstretched.

I wrap her in a hug and peck her on the forehead. "Good night," I say and close the door behind me.

I creep toward the kitchen and stand near the entrance.

"—it's alright. We can't do anything about it now, can we? Just let it go," Grandma says.

"I'm just saying that next time, I want to know. I want to be informed about my family. I deserve to know."

Grandpa nods.

"I heard that the Tatmadaw is coming," Mama announces.

Grandpa's and Uncle's heads perk up. "What?"

"I heard that the government sent the Tatmadaw and they'll be here soon. The neighbor's wife told me. They're going to leave the village tomorrow," Mama says.

"We aren't moving," Grandpa exclaims. "The Tatmadaw is coming due to the attacks. They won't do anything to us. They can't kill everyone in the village. That's impossible."

"But what if they do?" Grandma's voice quivers.

"They won't. They can't. Even though they hate us, they still abide by rules."

"Are you sure? It won't take long to pack up and we can always find a place somewhere else," Mama suggests.

"No, we're not leaving. Nothing will happen. I know it. You have to trust me," Grandpa says and the conversation stops.

CHAPTER 64

KAN

AS SOON AS you set foot out of the truck, your heart jumps. The village is peaceful, quiet. It's a place you would like to live in. It's a place you used to live in with Mama. You loved the quiet, the privacy. You've never liked the city. It's too busy, too crowded, too undisciplined.

Except it's infested with the Rohingya. They wander on the streets like stray rats hunting for anything to steal.

A fire ignites in your heart. You grip your rifle and glance down at your ghostly pale knuckles. You can't wait to watch the bullets rip through thin flesh, a thick river of dark red flowing through the streets.

Bennu taps on your shoulder. You bite your tongue to keep yourself from attacking the first Rohingya you see.

"The commander is talking," he whispers. You perk up.

"—attacks. Because of their crimes, you have full permission to extract compensation from the people of the village. But most importantly, if you find any of the people on the list, you can arrest them and bring them to the truck. They are the leaders and executioners of ARSA. We need to apprehend them at all costs."

Around you, the other cadets pass around pieces of paper. When it reaches your hands, you glare at the pictures laid out.

Ayub Omar.

Muhammad Khan.

Omar Ahmed.

Ali Asad.

Yunus (no last name documented).

Each one has the same expression, a solemn frown. The pictures were cropped from the regulation pictures since the edge of a white sign peeps out from the bottom.

You hand the paper to Bennu and close your fists. If you get your hands on any of these traitors, you will pound them and then drag them to the truck, barely alive.

That will be so satisfying.

A grin spreads on your face. You warp out of your imagination as the commander starts to speak again.

"Now, you may kill anyone you see, but it would be best if you would spare them. We don't want the UN to attack us. If you are ever interviewed about your role in this operation, state that this is a necessity. ARSA killed twelve police officers and attacked thirty posts. They thought they could get away with it. If we don't make them an example, other groups will attack us, leading to chaos. We are a peaceful government and we want to preserve the safety and peace of our citizens. Understand?"

A wave of heads salutes the commander. He nods, a hungry smile spreading on his face.

"You are dismissed."

CHAPTER 65

TAREK

I SIT DOWN, wiping the sweat from my face. I watch the clothes flap in the wind, beads of water dripping from them. Mama is crouched over the barrel, squeezing the soaking clothes.

I get up and reach for the bunch near her, gently pushing her away from the barrel.

"I got it," I say and savor the satisfying sound of squeezing clothes.

"You're supposed to be taking a break," she responds, trying to grab the shirt from my hands.

"I already took it."

"You sat for a minute. Let me do it."

I smile. "No, Mama. You need to take a break. You'll get tired."

A smile spreads on Mama's face. She sighs and goes inside. I watch her sit down on a cushion through the window. She catches me looking and smiles.

What I would do to see that smile every moment of my life.

Grrrr.

I stop squeezing and glance down toward the ground. My whole body starts to vibrate, my teeth clattering against each other.

I drop the shirt and dive into the house. Mama is standing up, her fingers white from gripping the wall. Her eyes are widened, screaming at me.

I throw open the front door. Outside, the blurs of people fly past the windows. Children are screaming and the adults are crying.

I turn back toward Mama. Everyone's in the living room. "We have to go," I yell.

"We can't. Not yet. We need to pack first," Grandma shrieks.

"We don't know what's going on. We have to leave *now*. Before it's too late," I say.

"No, we're not leaving," Grandpa affirms.

I open my mouth to say something, anything to get us out of here.

Crack. Tetete.

I slam into the ground, covering my head with my hands. Screams echo out throughout the village.

I grip my throbbing head and open my eyes. Grandpa and Grandma are slumped near a wall while Mama and Uncle huddle near each other. The fear in their eyes says everything.

"Run," Grandpa mouths and everyone shoots up.

"Where's Haya? *Where's Haya?*" I scream.

I burst into Mama's room and scoop the mass hidden in the blanket. She kicks, screams and bites like a feral cat in someone's arms.

"It's me. It's me."

A pair of tear-stricken eyes peer back at me from inside the blanket. Haya grips me with all her life, pulling herself up.

I grab her blanket and pull it around her.

"Don't. Let. Go," I command.

She holds on even tighter. I kick the front door open and barrel out the front door. Everyone's already outside, sacks of food, clothes and money in their arms.

Tetetete.

"Let'sgoLet'sgoLet'sgo!" Uncle screams. He throws a red backpack toward me and I grab it, running after him.

Behind us, people scream, their agonizing, pained sounds ringing in my ears. People dash past me, trying to get as far away from the sounds as possible.

The earth trembles as the familiar sound of boots stampede over them. Rifles load, the *click* deafening me. People beside me crumple to the floor as each shot is fired. A river of red flows from each street, pooling in the marketplace.

I stop at the sight of it all.

Crash.

Something crashes into me from behind. I wrap my arms around Haya, protecting her from the fall. I stay still for a split second before crawling as far away as possible.

A pair of lifeless, glass eyes stare at me. A stream of red trickles out of his mouth. Behind him, a wall of greenish-brown inches closer and closer, the black holes of the rifles laughing at me. A layer of orange licks at them, biting into the houses and trees all around.

I whimper, trying to get as far away as possible. A hand pulls me up and twirls me around.

"Keep going," Uncle says, pushing me ahead. I stumble forward, panting. The air is thick with blood and smoke, as if I can see the red and gray entering into my lungs.

I cough, vomit threatening to burst from my mouth.

"They're coming, *they're coming,*" Haya screams, digging her nails into my arm.

I force myself to keep going.

CHAPTER 66

KAN

YOU LOVE THE fear. You love the way it dances in their eyes. You love that they know the inevitable. That they know you'll take their life, even if you have to tear it out of them.

You watch as the boy under you has that same look of fear in his eyes. You aim your gun at his head, your finger ready at the trigger. The boy holds the clinging child tighter. You watch as he swallows hard.

Slam.

A hard object flies into you, knocking you off the boy. You allow yourself to crash to the ground before jumping back onto your feet.

You glare at the man in front of you. Before any of you have time to process what's going on, the barrel of your gun is on the man's temple. The man glances back at the boy, who is already several feet away.

You watch as he smiles a sad, welcoming smile. He turns back to you and a single tear drips down his cheek.

Crack.

The bullet flies out and rips through his skull. The man freezes for a second, sitting upright before falling face first onto the ground. His eyes are wide open, lifeless. His mouth hangs open and his legs are bent under him.

You glance toward Bennu and he grins at you. You smile back, your heart speeding up.

You get up and continue through the street, your gun loaded in your hand.

CHAPTER 67

TAREK

I GRIP MY knees and take a deep gulp of air for a second.

And then I continue running,
And running,
And running.
My heart pounds.
Thump.
Thump.
Thump.
I stumble over the fallen bodies scattered all over the ground. The brownish dirt is now streaked with red, turning into a thick mud.

I grip my stomach to keep myself from throwing up.

Ahead of me, Uncle, Mama and the rest of them run close to each other, glancing over their shoulders to check on me.

Weeee.

Weee.

Bullets fly right past me.

Splat. Crack.

Time stops.

Every twitch, every breath, I can see it.

Grandma crumples onto the floor like a piece of paper on fire. Grandpa rushes to her, shaking her. Tears form on the brink of his eyes.

I trip near them and crawl toward them. I grip Grandma's arm and I jerk backward.

There's nothing.

She's dead.

Haya screams, her words muffled. I try to focus, but it's like I'm drowning.

I grip Grandpa's arm and tug at it. "Come on," I yell.

"I can't. I can't," he cries.

I pull him hard and he drops to the ground, barely lifting his head. He places his hand on the dirt and pushes himself off.

But he instantly collapses.

I watch as the bullets rip through him. His arm goes limp and I shriek. Haya cries, screaming. She grips on my neck, choking me.

I kick off the ground and dart toward Mama. I glance over to the two bodies on the floor, their blood merging together.

My legs beg to stop, but I can't.

I can't.

I can't.

I catch up to Mama and Uncle. Mama's hand covers her mouth, and she blinks fast, trying to keep the tears from bursting out. Uncle holds her other hand, pulling her faster and faster.

A sharp scream pierces the air. I peer over my shoulder. Two soldiers drag a young woman by her hair. Bloodied scratches are painted over her face. She claws at their ankles, but they tug harder. She yelps in pain. Her nails dig into the dirt, but it's no use.

I force my head forward. My lungs burn, my heart pounding against my ribs. I can almost hear the *crack* coming as my heart threatens to rip out of my chest.

I wrap my arms around Haya to keep her from slipping. Darkness forms around the edges of my vision, but I force it away.

I have to keep going.

I have to keep running.

I have to keep moving.

Something barrels into me from the side. The air rushes out of me as I hit the ground. I try to open my eyes, but my head is spinning.

I rip open my eyes to see the barrel of a gun cackling at me. Just beyond it, there's a man, a boy about my age. His finger is on the trigger.

I freeze, my lips quivering.

A sick smile is planted on the boy's face.

He's enjoying this. He's enjoying the suffering.

He's enjoying the blood.

I wrap my arms around Haya, trying to protect her from the shot.

And then time stops.

My breathing stops.

My heart stops.

Uncle pounces on the soldier. He's caught off guard for a second before he aims at Uncle's head.

I jump off the floor.

"No."

Crack.

I try to pull Uncle away. I try to pull him back, away from the bullet. Right before it jams into his head, Uncle smiles at me. A sad, knowing smile.

He slumps onto the floor, his legs bent at an odd angle.

"Nonono."

I reach out, trying to feel the gentle *thump* of Uncle's heart, but it's silent.

Deathly silent.

I watch the boy load his rifle again.

I force myself up. Before the gun is aimed toward me, I'm running toward the forest, forcing myself not to look over my shoulder.

I force myself to flee from my home.

CHAPTER 68

KAN

YOU SPY THE woman from far away. She struggles to keep running, stopping frequently. She glances over her shoulder every so often and you pretend to be focused on a body near you.

You smirk every time she continues going. She doesn't even suspect you have your eyes on her. She stumbles and crashes into the ground.

You freeze, watching her vigilantly. She grips her ankle but forces herself forward. She turns left into an obscure street. You search left and right and then follow in, your heart accelerating.

. . .

The woman peers over her shoulder as she exits the street. You hide behind a house, shrouded in the shadows. She turns back toward the forest ahead of her.

You maintain a distance between the two of you, ducking behind trees and bushes when she stops.

You catch a glimpse of her fear-stricken eyes. Her pupils are thin and her breathing is hard. You can even hear the sharp intake of air several feet away.

The woman keeps on running deeper and deeper into the forest, diving into the greenery around. She turns right when she sees an impenetrable wall of plants.

She slows down to a walk after a few minutes and stops looking over her shoulder.

A mistake, if only she knew.

You creep closer.

The woman stops in front of a pond, a muffled sob escaping her lips. She looks at a mass in the pond. It's deformed and greenish, flies swarming all around it.

She doesn't hear you creep up right behind her.

You grip the knife in your belt and tiptoe until you're just a few inches away.

She turns around too late.

You slap your hand over her mouth, sliding the knife near her neck.

"Shh, you wouldn't want this knife to slice your throat, would you?" You whisper near her ear.

She freezes, her mouth quivering against your hand. You force her onto her knees, the knife still at her neck. You release your hand.

"Please—"

Slash.

You plunge the knife into her back. "I warned you not to talk," you spit.

She starts to weep, trying to control the sounds from her mouth.

Slash. Slash.

"I told you not to make any sounds."

At this point, the woman is on the floor, clutching her bleeding stomach. Her breathing is raspy like a deer that knows its fate once the lion sinks its jaws in.

You've always wanted to see the slight fear in the deer's right before it gives up.

You raise the knife up and bring it down.

Again,

And again.

And again.

CHAPTER 69

TAREK

THE AIR STARTS to clear up the closer I get to the forest. The few people left are huddled near the trees, hiding in the shadows. Many of them have their phones out, recording the destruction.

I lean against a tree and take in everything. Heavy, black smoke hangs over the village as orange devours the small homes and shops. On the buildings close to us, blood is painted all over. Near the bottom, there are red handprints. Wet bodies are scattered all over the dirt.

The dirt we used to play on. The dirt we used to laugh on. The dirt we used to build our home.

Now, it's layered with blood. Now, it's coated with the blood of innocent souls. Souls that were hated just because they were different, just because they weren't wanted.

I feel the tingle of water on my shirt. I glance down to find Haya's face buried into my stomach, sobs leaking from her.

I rub her back, trying to hold my own tears back. The people around me are hugging each other, crying into each other's shoulders. Cuts and bruises are streaked on their skin and their clothes are torn.

To my left, there's a man groaning on the floor. He grips his leg as his daughter tends to him. As soon as he releases his grip, a fountain of red sprouts from his leg. His daughter reaches into her bag and ties a shirt around her father's leg tightly.

He yelps in pain.

My chest tightens. My eyes comb through the groups of people.

This can't be right. I must be missing her.

I search through the crowds again and the air rushes out of my lungs.

Mama's not here.

CHAPTER 70

KAN

YOU'RE STUCK IN a cycle of rage. The fire inside you grows, licking at your insides and traveling through your veins.

The red, it's not enough to extinguish the fire. It's not enough to fill your thirst. Nothing is.

Color starts to fade and the red bleeds in, blinding you.

Everything is red.

It's so beautiful.

It's so alluring.

You stop to admire it. You crouch to the ground, getting as close as you can.

You can see the blood reaching out for you. You can see it calling to you.

And you want to respond.

You want it to devour you, to wrap its warm blanket around you.

Crack.

You whip around, your knife ready at your side. Everything is silent, the sound of your panting ringing in your ears.

"Who's there?" You bark.

Nobody responds.

You grind your teeth, remaining frozen in place, waiting for the threat. Waiting for the knife to sink into more flesh.

But nobody's there.

You turn back to the body. Your eyes are fixed on it. The precise, clean cuts everywhere.

It's a work of art. It's beauty.

The red is the drink of life. Without it, no one can live. With it, you can take. You can take from those who don't deserve to have it. You take from those who don't belong here.

You can take what belongs to you.

CHAPTER 71

TAREK

THUMP. THUMP. THUMP.

I try to take a deep breath but the air is tight, refusing to enter my lungs. I run my hands in my hair, tugging lightly to force me back into reality.

She has to be here somewhere. She was right here a minute ago. She's probably hidden among the people here.

But deep down, something tugs at you. Nervousness settles in your stomach.

What if she's not? What if she's not here? What if you and Haya are the only ones left?

I hoist Haya off me, even though she clings on.

"You have to walk now," I tell her gently and she finally gives in.

"Where's Mama?" she asks.

I try to keep my voice steady. "She's here somewhere."

"Are you sure?"

I nod, my stomach turning due to the lie.

"I'm going to go look for her. You stay here, alright?"

She grabs onto my leg before I can go. "No. No."

I comb the crowd with my eyes and spy a familiar face. I lift Haya up and make my way toward the man.

"Assalam Alaikum, Hasan."

He turns toward me, his eyes shining with recognition. "Walaikum Salam," he says quietly.

"Um, can you do me a huge favor please? I need someone to look after Haya while I search for Mama."

He nods but the heaviness in his eyes tells me what I don't want to believe. He knows she's not here. He knows that she's...gone.

I swallow hard. "Thank you," I say, my voice shaking.

I turn around, forcing myself to keep my tears inside. I swim through the loose crowds, hunting for the familiar blue hijab.

After weaving through people twice, I search deeper into the forest.

The surrounding green grows thicker, blocking the sunlight. The forest is dead silent.

Crack.

I freeze. My ears perk up to the faint sounds. I peer behind me.

Nobody.

I turn toward the sound and creep closer, lying low. I slowly part the leaves to find a soldier hacking at a body. His arm moves up and down within a blink and every time he brings the knife up, it rains red.

My lungs close and I fall backward. I try to move away but my feet are glued to the grass.

The body. I've seen the body somewhere. I focus on the scarf around the body's neck.

My stomach drops.

It's Mama.

Mama's dead.

And that soldier killed her.

CHAPTER 72

TAREK

THE SOLDIER JERKS backward as I fall onto a stick.

I freeze in place, hidden behind the intricate bushes. His eyes are sharp, crazed like he's been taken over.

Like he's not human anymore.

They resemble the eyes of a lion after it bites down into the neck of its prey, watching it bleed.

I muffle my gasp.

It's the same soldier who killed Uncle. It's the same soldier who tried to kill me.

My heart beats wildly, heat coursing through my veins.

Anger.

Raw anger.

I clench my teeth and force myself to remain calm. But it doesn't work.

A few seconds later, the soldier turns back to Mama, staring at her like she's a painting. He stares at the blood sprayed everywhere.

All of a sudden, he turns his sight to the pond. I follow his sight and stifle a gasp.

I strain to see the distorted lump in water. This is the pond we found Aunt in.

And this is the same place Mama was killed.

I clench my fists, trying to breathe, trying to cool myself down but I can't.

I can't control it.

It's taken over, slowly traveling through my blood and into my heart. I crouch down further, trying to focus. Trying to get a hold of myself.

The fire in the soldier's eyes has cooled down. He's still staring at the blood and every second he does, the *thumps* in my ears get louder and louder.

I want to reach out. I want to go to Mama. I want to hug her one last time.

But I can't.

I can't move from here or else the anger will take control.

Or else the rage will take control.

CHAPTER 73

TAREK

ALL OF A sudden, the soldier raises his knife over his head. I lose control and pounce out of the bushes, tackling him.

He topples to the ground, but he grabs my arm, pulling me down with him. I pin the knife-wielding hand but he pulls away. He rolls over, pushing me under him.

The glint of metal in the sun blinds me. I jerk to the side.

Smash.

The knife flies past my ear, landing in the grass next to me. The soldier pulls it out, the crisp sound of metal ringing in my ears.

"I couldn't get you last time but I will now," the soldier says, holding the knife high up.

I buck, pushing him off me and scramble to my feet.

He gets up and turns to me. The soldier's hair is disheveled. He glances toward his side where his helmet rests in the tall grass.

We remain frozen in place for a second before he charges at me.

I move to the side, pushing him away. He falls back but closes the gap between us. He swings with his knife.

I shield my face with my arms.

Slash.

It slices my arm, leaving a clean cut in my shirt. I grip the wound, biting my tongue to keep from screaming in pain.

My vision grows dark. The knife. Where's the knife?

Slice.

I jerk to the side, right before the soldier's arm strikes down. The force of the attack blows a gust of cold air into my face.

The soldier tries to slash me from above but I grab his hand. He pushes down as I struggle to keep the blade away from me.

I twist his arm. The boy yelps in pain, instantly dropping the knife.

I try to force my eyes ahead, trying not to glance toward the gun on his belt.

When I look into the soldier's face, all I see is fury and hate. His eyes are narrowed and red, his eyebrows shading the white in his eyes. His teeth are clenched while his nose flares. His chest rises up and down, his nose inflated.

The soldier growls before charging at me again. He slams his fist into my face, my bone cracking. I rub my jaw.

I stumble backward, landing on the grass. The soldier pounces, his knees holding my arms in place.

"Now, you're my prey," he cackles.

I try to lift my arms, I try to buck, I try to throw him off but he's too strong. The soldier lifts his arm up, his fist blocking the sun.

Smack. Smack. Smack.

He pounds on my face. Flashes of pain shoot up from my cheeks and they tingle.

The soldier climbs off me. I try to scramble back to my feet but a boot buries itself into my stomach. I crumple inward, my arms hugging my abdomen.

Thunk. Thunk.

He kicks again and again. My mouth fills with metal and I puke onto the grass. Red coats the dark green.

The soldier steps back, ready to kick me again. I roll away, jumping to my feet. As he charges forward, I do too.

My fist meets with his jaw within a second.

The soldier jerks backward, his eyes widened. His face morphs into anger and he propels forward again.

Crack.

Smash.

Thud.

I grip the boy by his shirt. He thrashes in my grip.

"You think you can get away with hurting my mother?" I spit.

A sickening grin spreads on his lips. "The red sustains me. The blood gives me life. And she *deserved* it."

I slam the soldier to the ground, jumping onto him.

But I freeze.

He doesn't move. I expect him to fight back but he's not moving.

I shudder.

He's not breathing.

I scramble off him, crawling as far as I can. Blood pools around the soldier's head. His eyes are wide open, the life sucked from them.

I grip my head.

He's dead.

He's dead.

He's dead.

And I killed him.

CHAPTER 74

TAREK

I KILLED SOMEONE.

I glance down at my hands, imagining blood painted on them. I crawl backward until something wet spreads on my pants.

I look down, at the lake of blood under me. I fall forward, the soft grass tickling my face.

I scramble onto my feet. The sky is bright, some clouds dotting the sky. A stream of black climbs to the sky, hints of smoke in the air here.

I slow my breathing and close my eyes. *I'm dreaming. Nothing's going wrong. I'm at home, in the kitchen. I'm eating dinner with everyone.*

My lungs open up. I open my eyes, crouching near Mama's body.

I stifle a hiccup. "I'm sorry, Mama. I'm so sorry. I should have noticed you were missing. I should have turned. This is all my fault. You're dead because of me. Please forgive me."

I wipe my eyes. "I'm sorry I wasn't the son you dreamed of. I'm sorry I was caught up in my own dreams. I'm sorry I was sleeping when you needed me at night, when all the nightmares used to come. I'm sorry I couldn't be there for you when Papa died. And—" I gulp. "I'm sorry for killing someone. If you knew, you wouldn't be able to look me in the eyes. I'm sorry for being so reckless with that soldier's life. He was my age, but I took his life away. I'm so, so sorry."

I place my head down on the grass and my legs give way. I squeeze the blades of green in my hands, the sobs uncontrollable.

"I'm so, so, so sorry. I'm so sorry I never told you how much I love you. I'm sorry I didn't hug you enough. I'm sorry I didn't massage your sore feet enough. I'm sorry for being a bad son. I'm sorry. I'm sorry. I'm sorry." I wheeze. "I'm sorry."

I lay there for a few minutes. The sun creeps to its bed when I finally warp back to reality.

You need to go back to Haya. She's alone.

I lift my heavy heart up and drag myself through the forest. I glance back one last time at Mama. I wipe my eyes and stare up at the sky, trying to stop the tears.

Haya can't see me like this. I need to be there for her. I'm the only one left for her. She can't see me broken.

I take a step forward, ripping myself from the ropes of grief holding me back.

CHAPTER 75

TAREK

I DRAG MYSELF through the green, emerging into the brown dirt. The scattered crowd of people are still there. I turn to the right, spotting Hasan's grayish head among everyone else.

Haya's on the ground, her back against a tree. Her hair is disheveled, spots of blood dotting her face. Her eyes are a raw red as if they haven't closed in over a week.

She traces her finger in the dirt. I crouch down next to her, leaning my head against the tree.

She doesn't even notice me. I pick her up. Haya screams and claws, her eyes closed.

"Shh, it's me. It's me." I wrap my arms around her tightly and she calms down.

The people staring at me turn back to their families. There is a slight *buzz* around us, the sounds of crying, whispers and painful groans.

Some of them gather in the middle, forming a ring. Hasan gestures for me to come. I lift Haya up and walk there.

"We can't stay here," one of the elders says.

"But we can't leave," Salma's mother exclaims.

"We have to. They've destroyed everything. Our homes are ashes, our families are dead and all of our belongings are gone. We don't know how long the soldiers will be here. We're not wanted here. They've made it clear. We need to go somewhere where we are accepted."

Silence shrouds us. A lump forms in my throat.

I can't leave. I can't. I can't leave Mama lying in the grass. I can't leave Uncle, Grandpa and Grandma in the village. I can't leave Aunt rotting in the pond. I can't leave my family.

A small hand tugs on my shirt. I peer down toward Haya.

"Are we really going to leave?" she whispers.

"I don't know," I respond.

"I don't want to."

"I know but...we don't have a choice."

"Where's Mama?" she asks.

The air chokes me. I don't respond. Haya's eyes flood with tears and she buries her face into my shirt.

I dab my eyes and focus on the conversation. Everyone around me is nodding. Within a second, the group disbands, scattering to their corners.

Whispers start and people begin to pack their things. I freeze, gulping for air.

We can't leave. We can't.

Hasan squeezes my shoulder. "Pack your things. We're leaving."

He watches as a single tear drips down my cheek. "I know you don't want to but we don't have a choice. Come on. Where's your stuff?" he says softly.

I turn to look at my back but there's nothing where the once red backpack was.

I glance toward Hasan. He smiles. "It's alright. We'll share."

I walk robotically with Hasan, my mind numb. I squeeze my arm where the soldier sliced it.

A wet spot spreads on my shirt and I glance down. Haya is still sobbing. I rub her back and let her.

People start to gather at the entrance of the forest. I trudge toward them. Once the last person is packed, we disappear into the forest.

I glance behind at the village one last time. I watch as it recreates itself, the echoes of laughter, talk and joy radiating from within.

I blink, the illusion evaporating. Now, it's burned to the ground, the stench of blood and death reeking within it.

I turn back to look forward as my heart sinks into my stomach.

We don't have a home anymore. Memories are the only thing left but even those hurt to think of.

PART III:

AFTER

CHAPTER 76

TAREK

THE THICK STENCH of smoke gradually fades as we trudge deeper into the forest. The grass *crunches* beneath us. Every time there's a single sound, everyone freezes.

I hold on to Haya tightly. I hate living in this fear. I hate living like animals, searching for predators.

The path grows familiar. Ahead, I spy the glint of sunlight shining from the ground. The pond grows crisp.

I suck in a breath and turn, shielding Haya's eyes. Gasps erupt from ahead.

"Poor woman."

"She didn't deserve that."

"Who would do that?"

The whispers peck at me, igniting a small fire. All I want is to keep on moving.

We inch forward. I try to force my eyes away, but they wander to Mama's body, soaked in blood.

I shudder.

A few feet ahead, I spy the boots of the soldier, lying on the grass. I turn my head.

I can't look at him. I can't look at someone I killed. Someone whose blood is on my hands.

. . .

As soon as the sun peeks out from behind the trees, my eyes jerk open. Haya is fast asleep next to me, her chest gently rising up and down.

I slowly sit up. Haya stirs, mumbling something inaudible before gently snoring again.

I step over her and sit next to the people already awake.

"Here." Hasan hands me a piece of bread and a small piece of fish. I put the food down.

"It's for you. Your sister will get some too, but you need to eat to walk."

I swallow the vomit climbing up my throat and force myself to eat. It's been almost a whole day since I last ate. I devour the dry food, my stomach growling for more.

"Alright, we need to wake everyone up. We need to keep moving," a man says as he gets up.

"Haya, Haya. Time to wake up." I shake her shoulders. Her eyes flutter open.

"I don't want to," she cries.

I lift her and rest her head against my shoulder, patting her back until she's asleep again. It's best if she's asleep. It'll be easier for the both of us.

I pick up the pack Hasan gave me and sling it over my other shoulder. A few minutes later, we're walking again. Everyone is silent, mourning our village and the families we left behind.

What I would do to be in our home, eating breakfast with Grandpa. What I would give to hug everyone again. What I would give to hug Mama one more time.

Just one more time.

"Where are we going?" A woman asks from the back.

Others nod, echoing the same question. Someone from the front answers. "I've heard that Indonesia is accepting refugees. Let's go there."

No one objects. "But how are we going to get there?"

"We'll have to cross the sea," a man says. "I've done it before. It's not difficult. After that, when we reach land, they'll accept us and we'll continue on with our lives."

"But what if they don't accept us?" the woman asks.

No one answers. No one wants to face the idea of being rejected. No one wants to face the idea of not being wanted.

CHAPTER 77

TAREK

A THICK LAYER of sweat coats my body. I switch the arm holding Haya and wipe the dripping beads down my forehead. A swarm of mosquitoes follows us, biting every piece of bare skin. I force myself to ignore the burning red sores on my arms.

"Mhm." Haya stirs. She lifts her head and rubs her eyes with her small hands. "Where are we?"

"I don't know," I respond.

Her bottom lip trembles and her eyes glisten.

I muster the best smile I can. "But don't worry. We'll be near the sea soon. We're almost there."

Her eyes dry up slightly and she gently pushes my shoulder. "I want to walk."

I stop on the side and help her down. I hold my hand out and she holds onto it. She doesn't say anything else.

Soon, the only sounds are the *thud* of footsteps. As I glance around, everyone has heavy, downcast eyes. It's as if life has been sucked out of everyone. We're hollow beings now, programmed to keep walking without uttering a single word.

Something tugs on my arm and I'm pulled down slightly. I turn to find Haya on the ground. She's examining her hands. On the ground underneath her, there are a few spots of tears.

I heft her up and she cries silently. "I'm hungry," she whispers.

"I'll ask someone if they have some food."

I turn to the woman next to me. "Excuse me?"

She doesn't respond.

"Excuse me?"

"Hm?"

"Do you have some food to spare? My sister is hungry, and I don't have any."

Her eyes narrow. "I have children to feed too. You can't just ask people and expect them to give you their food. We're barely making it through and you have the audacity to ask us?"

I swallow the rock in my throat. "I-I'm sorry. I didn't—"

A finger taps on my shoulder from behind me. I whip back to see Hasan holding out half a piece of bread.

I smile, tears pricking my eyes. "Thank you," I croak.

He smiles at me. He turns to the woman. "We're *all* starving and tired here. We're *all* coming from the same destruction. All we have is each other. It would be best that it stays that way."

The woman turns red. "I'm sorry," she says to me.

I muster a smile and nod.

CHAPTER 78

TAREK

"I SEE WATER. I see water!" someone from the front shouts.

A surge of people floods to the front. I'm swept up with them. In front of us, red light glints in the clear water. The orangish-red sun peeks out from the horizon, sinking beneath the water.

"We're finally here," people exclaim and for the first time, a blanket of joy settles on us. A smile blooms on my face.

We're finally done walking. We'll finally be safe.

We'll finally be free.

"Is that the ocean?" Haya asks.

I nod.

"Wow," she whispers, admiring the sea. "It's pretty."

I chuckle. "It is. It really is."

"Alright, everyone. May I have your attention," the man who was guiding us through the forest says. He ascends on a log, slightly elevating himself. Everyone turns their heads toward him. "Get a good night's sleep. Tomorrow, we'll board a boat and make our way to Indonesia. We'll leave as soon as the sun rises."

Everyone nods and a hush of silence descends on us. Even though no one is saying anything, the smiles on their faces speak a thousand words.

I set Haya down near a tree and unroll the cloth in my pack. Haya runs her hand through her hair and smells herself. She pouts.

I stretch my sore back. "Let's go wash ourselves in the water."

Her face lights up and she jumps up. I hold my hand out and she pulls me toward the sea.

I laugh. "Wait, wait. I have to tell Hasan first."

She turns, still tugging me behind her, toward Hasan. He turns toward us and smiles when he sees Haya.

"We're going to wash up in the water. We'll be back before it gets dark."

He hesitates. "Alright. But please be careful. Make sure you don't go too deep. The waves can be strong. And make sure you come back before dinner."

I nod and tug on Haya's hand before Hasan changes his mind. We step into the sand. I stand there for a second, savoring the warmth under my sinking feet.

I inhale the salty air. Haya pulls on my hand.

"Hurry. It'll be dark soon."

"Alright, alright," I chuckle.

A few steps later, the cool water crashes against our feet. We wade into the water until it reaches Haya's knees.

"This is as far as we can go. Now hurry up and wash up," I tell her.

Haya lets go of my hand and sits down in the water, submerging everything except her head.

"Can you wash my hair?" she asks.

I nod. She lays her head down on the surface of the water and I massage her scalp, trying to get rid of all the dirt.

"I think that's enough," I say after a minute. She starts to wash her face.

I lie down in the water, trying to submerge my body into the water. I barely fit in. I comb my hair in the water and after I emerge from the water, I rub my body, scraping the dirt off.

The water around me starts to turn dark and murky. The sun is barely peeking over the horizon, a slight line of red over the black.

"Time to go." I lift Haya out of the water and we trudge back to the camp. I rub my aching arms and back.

Everyone is gathered around a fire, huddled close. Hasan's eyes relax when he sees me and he gestures at the empty space next to him.

When we sit, he hands us each a piece of bread and some fish. I nod, smiling tiredly.

.   .   .

The gentle song of the crickets lulls me to sleep. But as soon as the darkness creeps in, my vision turns red. There's blood everywhere.

I stir, not wanting to open my eyes.

Aaaaahhh. Aaaaaahhh.

I shoot up at the sound of sharp screaming, grasping my ears. A few others wake up as well and they're all glaring at me.

I glance down toward Haya and scoop her up.

"Shhh. Shhh. It's okay. It's okay. It's just a nightmare. I've got you," I whisper, rubbing her back.

Her eyes flutter closed, and she rests her head against my stomach. I continue rubbing her back, leaning against the tree.

CHAPTER 79

TAREK

MY EYES DON'T close after Haya's nightmare. My brain begs me to sleep, but I can't. I just can't.

Soon, streaks of orangish-pink paint the sky. The guide, Zaid, is the first one up. He proceeds to wake some others up.

"We need to leave soon. Hurry."

I rub my eyes, trying to wipe the sleep from them. I place Haya on the mat and pack everything else. The food, the water bottles, money.

By the time I finish, everyone is bustling around. There's a slight fear in the air. The fear of the unknown. The fear of everything going wrong.

I catch Hasan observing us. He nods when he catches my eye. His eyes are darker than they usually are.

The fear has taken over them.

After I finish packing, I sling the bag over my shoulder. I lift Haya off the ground and lay her head on my shoulder.

She shuffles, but her muscles relax after a few seconds.

"Everyone done packing?" The guide asks. I nod, along with everyone else.

"Where's the boat?" Hasan asks.

Zaid swallows. "We'll have to walk the shoreline to find one. I tried to reach one of my contacts, but there's no signal there. We'll have to find a dock."

Someone grumbles. When I turn to examine the crowd, their faces are white.

"We're tired of walking," a woman shouts.

"I know. We all are," Zaid responds calmly. "But we have to manage with what we've got. We don't have the resources. I'm trying my best to make this as quick as possible, so please, bear with me."

The woman mumbles something.

"Alright, if there are no more concerns, let's go."

I force myself steady. My head is pounding and my legs feel like the ocean water. I inhale through my nose, straightening my back.

I have to keep going. I can't be weak right now. The weak are those snatched first. The weak are the targets. I have to keep moving.

We walk along the beach. It's the same landscape, the same scorching sun, the same glistening water. It's as if we've been in the same place since we began walking. Up ahead, it's the same scenery. Not a single boat or dock in sight.

My stomach flutters. I try to push it to the side, but it intensifies. Doubt pricks my heart. What if we can't find a boat? What if the owner of the boat isn't willing to let us use it? What if the Tatmadaw finds us first?

The air in my lungs tightens. I try to focus on the sand, but it's difficult. Haya turns her head away from the sun and groans quietly. I hide inside my thoughts, waiting for the aching to go away.

CHAPTER 80

TAREK

RIP.

A sharp jolt of pain radiates from my foot. I stumble, shooting my foot up. The bottom of my shoe is punctured, a ring of purple seeping around it. I peel my shoe off to examine the cut.

Beside me, people keep walking. I touch the scratch on my foot.

Not the worst cut ever.

I scan my surroundings until my eyes land on a large, green leaf near me. I reach out and rip it off the plant. I limp to the water and dip the leaf into it. Hopefully this will be enough to wash the dirt and germs off it.

I let it dry and place it on the sole of my shoe. It's uncomfortable, but it's better than allowing sand to enter the scratch. I speed walk to catch up with the group.

The landscape still doesn't change. The sun climbs up to the sky, towering over us. A few hours later, it starts to sink beneath the horizon. The leaf in my sole crumples, poking my foot. I try to take my mind off it.

"Is that a dock?" someone asks. Everyone straightens up, trying to get a look.

"It is," another confirms. People run toward it. I'm swept up in the crowd. Haya grips onto me tightly as I speedwalk with everyone.

"Everyone. *Everyone,*" Zaid shouts.

The group freezes.

"We have to remain calm. I'll go talk to the owner and see what he can do. It's best that all of us don't show up. In that time, set up camp. We can't leave at night. The sea is dangerous at night."

"I'll go with you," Hasan offers and Zaid nods.

"Everyone set up and we'll be back with the news."

My heart jumps at the sight of the boats rocking on the sea. We'll be out of this country soon. We'll finally be free soon.

I set Haya down on the mat and lean against a tree. My limbs finally relax, the fatigue settling in. My eyes scream for me to close them while my stomach shrieks for food. I haven't eaten anything since morning.

I wipe the pool of water on my face. I smell horrible, but my body refuses to move to wash myself. I can't.

Two men gather dry sticks while the women set up the ring of rocks. Soon, a raging orange is roaring to life. We huddle close to the warmth, my muscles savoring it.

A woman passes around some bread and fish. I devour it without even thinking.

"Look, there they are," a woman shouts, the joy laced in her voice. Two black figures inch closer and closer and soon, their crisp faces are clear in the light.

"What did they say?" The woman asks.

Zaid puts on a smile. "There's no one there. I'll try in the morning," he says. Beside him, Hasan is serious, his eyes gray.

My stomach flutters. I can see right through that smile. It's all an act. And Hasan's grim expression is sending chills down my spine.

He catches my eye, but he doesn't acknowledge it. He turns away from me.

You're overthinking. Why would they have anything to hide? Everyone's tired and it's difficult to be optimistic in this situation.

I nod, agreeing with the thought. I'm just paranoid.

Haya tugs on my sleeve. "Can I sleep?" she asks.

I nod and turn back to the fire.

"Can you come with me?" she whispers.

I grunt as I get up. The mat calls to me, luring me toward it. Haya settles in first, and then I do. She hugs my arm, leaning her cheek against it. The instant her eyes close, mine collapse. My mind cracks open, allowing the starry night to flood in.

CHAPTER 81

TAREK

THE SCREAMS JERK me awake again. A few people turn and cover their ears, but no one sits up. I lift Haya off the ground, cradling her.

"I'm right here. I'm right here," I croak, my mind begging for more sleep. I lean against the tree and rest my head against the bark. Soon, the world turns into a fuzz and then black.

. . .

Sturdy hands shake me awake. "Tarek? Wake up. We're going to leave soon."

"Alright," I mutter, my eyes barely open.

All I want is to go home, go into my bed. All I want is for this to be a dream, for this to be my imagination. All I want is to be a toddler again, huddled in Mama's lap. All I want is for her to sing me a lullaby and rock me to sleep. I want a warm glass of milk. I want Grandma's cooking. I want Uncle's laughter. I want Mama's smile. I want Grandpa's scratchy beard. I want Aunt's soft voice. I want it all back. That's all I want. Is that too much? Is that too much for me? Do I not deserve even a family? Do I not even deserve love, joy?

A tear streams down my cheek as I peer up at the sky, trying to hide it. I heft Haya up and limp toward the gathering of people. The hope on their faces is undeniable.

Zaid and Hasan stand in front of everyone. Hasan's lips hang in an upside down 'U.' The tingling returns.

"When are we going to leave?" A man asks from the crowd.

I watch the guide gulp. "As soon as possible," he mutters, his voice raspy.

"Can we leave now?" A woman asks.

"We have to figure something out first," Zaid hesitates, "I spoke to the owner of the dock. He's willing to lend us a boat but...but he's asking for money."

"We can all pool our money together. It should be enough," a girl around my age suggests.

"He's asking for money per person."

People begin to whisper, their eyes darting side to side with fear.

"Per person?" the girl asks.

Zaid nods solemnly.

"But not all of us have money," a man says.

"That's the problem. Some of us...won't be able to go." Zaid winces as the words echo throughout the camp.

People's eyes widen, some heavy with tears. "What about those who can't go?" I ask.

"They'll have to figure it out. Most likely, they'll go to Bangladesh," Zaid responds.

They, not we. He's going on the boat. But what about us? We won't know which way to go.

My heart pounds against my ribs.

Thump. Thump. Thump.

"Everyone who has money, go to the left. Everyone who doesn't, stay where you are."

A boulder lodges in my throat and tears threaten to flood the dam. My lungs tighten. Someone grabs my hand and pulls me away from the group. I blink, but the figure is fuzzy.

They let go of my hand. Something crinkles in my hand. I rub it and my vision crispens. I glance down toward my hand, at the small pile of money in my hand.

I lock eyes with Hasan. He smiles sadly. I shake my head and step toward him.

"Stop," he mouths. He walks toward me. "You need the money. You have to take care of her."

He gestures toward Haya, still asleep. "You need the money more than I do. You have your whole life ahead of you. I'm just an old man with a few years left."

"No. This isn't fair. This, this is *your* money. You need it," I croak. A glass bead drips down my face.

He chuckles. "My son, I promised myself that I would do everything in my power to protect you and your sister. This is me fulfilling my promise. If I take the money, it will kill me."

"But if I accept the money, it'll kill *me*."

"No, not accepting it will. The soldiers will come for you and will slaughter you mercilessly. Imagine your sister's pain if she's the only one who survives? You have to go on that boat." Hasan's eyes glint in the light.

I open my mouth to say something, anything but my tongue is heavy and grainy. The rock in my throat refuses to budge. My hand weighs down, the weight of the money pulling it down. My feet sink into the ground, my legs frozen in place.

Hasan turns around and settles into the group who can't go. I try to call out to him, but my lips are glued shut.

"It's okay," he mouths and smiles.

I shake my head. His smile widens, but the water in his eyes tells a different story.

CHAPTER 82

TAREK

"LET'S GO, EVERYONE," Zaid announces. He walks down the shoreline.

I glance behind toward Hasan. He nods, gesturing for me to look forward. I turn around with a heavy heart. Haya snores quietly, her tiny fingers wrapped around my sleeve.

I linger in the back of the group, dragging myself through the sand. The hole in my shoe has spread, my shoe about to rip in half.

On the dock, a stocky man stands on the edge. He turns when he hears our thundering footsteps. A white roll sticks out from his mouth, slightly black from the tip.

"Hmh," he grunts and holds out a bag. Zaid goes first, dumping some bills into the bag. The line inches forward until the brown bag is cackling at me. I toss the heavy bills into the bag and step into the boat.

It *creeeaks* with the weight. I scan the area and settle into a corner, laying Haya down on our mat. More people step onto the boat, gathering at the end closest to the shore.

I walk toward the back of the boat, glancing back to make sure Haya's still asleep. A crowd has gathered on the beach, the frowns on their faces sending chills down my spine. Hasan is at the front, smiling sadly. I wave and he perks up.

He waves back as soon as the boat sets off. I stumble backward, caught off guard by the movement. I look toward Hasan for the last time and walk back toward Haya, the infinite blue around us growing.

CHAPTER 83

TAREK

THE AIR SMELLS faintly like salt. There's blue everywhere. The sky is clear, not a single white dot anywhere. The sound of gentle waves crashing against the side of the boat calms me down, relief showering on me.

I sit on the floor, leaning against the tiny wall. Haya is peering over it, admiring the ocean.

"Make sure you don't fall in," I tell her.

"Do you think I'll see animals?" she asks, her eyes wide with hope.

I chuckle. "Maybe."

"Do you think I'll see a whale? Or maybe a dolphin?" She jumps with excitement.

"I don't know. You might see something."

She sits next to me and sighs. "Do you think everyone is happy in heaven?"

"What do you mean everyone?" I ask.

"Mama, Uncle, Grandpa, Grandma, Aunt," she pauses for a second, "Papa."

My heart lurches and I smile. "Yes, I think they're really happy there."

"But...are they still happy even if we're not there?" she asks.

"They're waiting for us. They'll be even happier when we're there."

"How do you know?"

I hug her. "I just know."

"Will I know when I'm older?"

I smile and kiss her hair. "Yes, you will."

.   .   .

I watch as night pulls its blanket over the sun, the stars' excitement shining across the sky. Haya points toward it. "It's so pretty," she whispers.

I nod and lie down next to her, barely fitting on the mat. Haya continues to admire the sky. Her eyes begin to flutter closed and she turns toward me, hugging my arm.

I put my other arm under my head, my eyes still wide open. I survey the boat. A few people hang near the wall, vomiting frequently. Some of the older men take turns with the propeller, the others sleeping.

I force my eyes closed, trying to go to sleep. But my mind is buzzing with life. And the worst part is, the demons of the past are out at night. I force my mind blank, trying not to think about the massacre.

Trying not to think about the blood.

But eventually, the demons win. They always do.

They infect my thoughts like poison. The images of everyone's bodies surface. I can smell the smoke, the blood. I can hear the screams, the gunshots. I can see the destruction, the death.

But I can't feel anything. I'm numb like a ghost.

That's what happens when there's so much pain. You stop feeling it.

The darkness swoops in after hours, lingering on the edges. I welcome it in, allowing it to take control of me.

CHAPTER 84

TAREK

ALL AROUND ME, there's darkness. I can't even see the ground underneath me. I hold my arms out, trying to feel around.

My foot hits something and I crouch, searching with my hands. They brush against an ice-cold object.

"What is this?" I mutter.

Click.

Suddenly, everything is white. I shield my eyes, adjusting to the brightness of it all. I glance down and squint at the dark, long object near me.

My vision grows crisp and I jerk back in horror. A scream threatens to break out of my throat.

Blood.

I glance toward my hand,

I touched a body.

I just touched a body.

I rub my hand against the dirt, as if that will wash the feeling away.

Thump. Thump. Thump.

My mind begs to go back. Ahead of me, bodies are scattered on the ground. I try to steady my breathing.

A scream pierces the air. I try to move but my feet refuse. I peer down to see a quarter of my legs in the ground.

I claw at the ground, trying to pull myself out. The screaming continues, growing more and more hoarse.

I close my eyes, trying to make out the words.

"Tarek. *Tarek.*"

I gasp. Haya. "I'm coming. I'm coming."

I tug, thrash and struggle but I sink deeper into the ground. My stomach is halfway in.

"They're coming, Tarek. They're coming."

I clench my teeth and try to pull myself up. "I'm coming," I yell.

Silence.

I stop struggling.

"Haya? *Haya?*"

Complete, deathly silence.

I jerk awake. The boat rocks gently underneath me and the sky is still dark blue. I'm on the boat. I'm safe. I'm not there. It was just a nightmare.

But then why does everyone say dreams can come true? If dreams can come true, so can nightmares, right?

I shudder, ignoring the voice in my mind. It was my imagination. Nothing more. It's not reality.

I turn toward Haya, watching her face morph into fear. I rub her back, whispering in her ear.

"Shh, shh. I'm right here. It's just a dream. It's a dream."

She relaxes slightly but the terror on her face doesn't disappear.

.   .   .

"Land. There's land," Zaid exclaims. Everyone clamors toward the front of the boat.

"He's right," a woman cries. The crowd erupts with cheers.

Haya's eyes flutter open and she examines the crowd. "What's going on?" she asks.

"They've spotted land," I respond, smiling.

She beams. "So we're done with the boat ride? We're going to get off?"

I nod. She holds her arms up. "I want to see."

I hoist her up and she squints to see the green line on the water. "Yay," she exclaims and hugs me.

I laugh.

The green line soon turns into a beach and then, the boat gently hits the dock there. Zaid wraps a rope around one of the poles and sets the wood plank.

No one waits for even a second. They dash off the boat, the joy pasted on their faces. I step off the wobbling boat and onto stable land. I can't believe it. We made it. We're finally free. We're finally safe.

Zaid walks toward an office on the dock. An officer emerges from inside to greet him. I watch as they talk, their mouths moving in incomprehensible forms.

Zaid's face drops and my heart lurches. He nods toward the officer and trudges back toward us. The frown on his face is unmistakable.

He clears his throat when he reaches us. "May I have everyone's attention please?"

The talking doesn't stop.

"Excuse me?" he asks, gently.

A hush falls over everyone.

"We're going to stay here for the night. There will be a refugee officer here tonight. They'll give us further instructions then. In the meantime, everyone get your things off the boat and set up camp on the beach. I need a few people to help me clean the boat to return it to the owner."

Some people nod, others simply go toward the boat. I touch the pack on my shoulder. I packed before getting off the boat. A few have also done the same.

Zaid gestures toward the beach. We follow him off the wooden dock, my feet savoring the warm sand. The air smells fresh and sweet, compared to the heavy, smelly air on the boat. Trees dot the beach, thickening the farther my eyes reach.

Haya releases from me, sliding down to the ground. She skips toward the shade. I smile, glancing over to the sea behind me. The sea that separates us from our home. The sea that separates me from my family.

I force myself to turn forward, to look toward a peaceful future but the chains of the past cling onto me.

"I'm hungry," Haya says once I reach the shade.

"I know but we have to wait for the sun to set. We don't have that much food," I respond.

She pouts. "There's nothing to eat right now?"

I shake my head. "Don't worry. I'm hungry too. Maybe the officer will bring some food when he comes. We just have to wait."

Haya sighs and leans against the tree. "Can I wash myself in the water?" she asks with hopeful eyes.

I peer at the scorching sun. "Let's wait until the sun is lower. It's hot right now and I don't want you to get sick."

"Okay," she mutters, her attention toward the sand. She lays down on her stomach, her legs moving up and down. She draws little figures in the sand with her finger, absorbed in their world.

"What are you drawing?" I ask, scooting closer to her.

"Nothing," she responds.

"That has to be something. What is it?"

"A gun," she replies without a second's hesitation. I freeze.

"A-A gun?"

She nods. "These are the soldiers. That's our house," she says.

"Alright. And what are the soldiers doing?"

"They're killing everyone."

I nod, processing everything. This is how she's coping with everything. She's trying to process what happened.

I let her continue drawing, focusing on the waves reaching in and out. My eyes beg to close. It's as if weights are pulling them down.

I turn my head. *It's alright if I close my eyes for just a minute.* The bright light outside turns into shadows, my body floating away.

CHAPTER 85

TAREK

THE SUN IS soon napping, the last rays of light slowly retreating.

"Can I wash myself now?" Haya asks, her eyes sparkling.

I nod and she skips toward the water. I stay under the tree for a few more seconds before forcing myself to walk toward the sea.

I sit in the water, savoring the soft coolness. I peer at my skin. Patches of red are all over my hands and legs. I run my hands over my neck and face. It's rough and my nose is peeling. My lips are cracked and no amount of licking helps.

I lie down in the water, soothing the sunburns and aches. The tension melts away.

I scrub my hair and body but no matter how hard I try, I feel dirty.

It's as if the soldier's blood is still there.

It's as if my family's blood is still there.

It's as if my home's ashes are still there.

I give up and continue sitting there, watching as Haya hums to herself. I can still see the grief, the sadness in her sparkling blue eyes.

The darkness starts to flood in. "Time to go," I mutter and scoop Haya up. I savor the warm tingling on my feet as I trudge through the sand.

Up ahead, a fire roars, people gathering around. A few people inch toward us from a distance.

Zaid stands up and makes his way toward them.

Haya tugs on my shirt. "When are we going to eat?"

I shrug, my eyes still locked on Zaid and the four other people. My stomach tingles. A few minutes later, they make their way closer.

As soon as they're a few feet away, I make out bags in each of their hands. My heart jumps and for a split second, I allow myself to hope.

Hope is all I have left.

Everyone shifts their attention to the approaching strangers. Zaid stops in front of us. His eyebrows are furrowed and the wrinkles around his mouth are more prominent. I can see the glint of tears in his eyes.

"Everyone," his voice cracks, "These are volunteers who brought us food and water for the night."

"When will we be able to get off the beach?" A woman asks.

Zaid takes a shaky breath. "We won't."

Everyone stops moving.

One of the volunteers speaks up. "The government won't allow you to enter Indonesia. I'm sorry," he mutters.

"But—But why?" I ask, a boulder lodging in my throat.

"I'm sorry but they're not accepting refugees currently."

My breathing grows shallow and the corners of my eyes turn black.

"But the government has given you food, water and other necessities to aid you on your journey back."

The words echo in my head.

Journey back.

Journey back.

Journey. Back.

"You'll—you'll have to leave tomorrow," the other volunteer says. The pain in her voice stabs me.

My chest weighs down, as if someone placed a thousand pounds on it. The volunteers nod toward Zaid and place their bags on the sand. They turn and walk back in the direction they came from.

Zaid remains frozen. We all do as the reality becomes clear.

They're really sending us back. They really don't want us. Nobody wants us.

We're alone.

CHAPTER 86

TAREK

I RIP MY eyes away from the shoreline, fighting back tears. My blood is boiling.

How can a human being send refugees away? How? And the fact that they thought they could make that up by giving us extra supplies?

Haya bumps into me as the boat starts moving. Her eyes are widened, glistening in the hot sun. She bites her lip, a fat tear forming in her eyes.

I lift her up, searching her eyes. "It's okay. It's okay. Maybe it's a good idea to go to Bangladesh. Mama mentioned she had a cousin there."

"I don't want to be here," she hiccups, "I want to go home."

I swallow. "I know. I want to, too."

"Why can't we go back home?"

"We'll be safer somewhere else. And home is where the family is. As long as we're together, we'll have a home, no matter where we are."

She's quiet for a few seconds. "I want Mama," she whispers.

"I want her too."

"Can you take me to her?"

I freeze. "I—She—I can't."

"Why?"

"She's in a better place, remember?" I respond.

Haya doesn't say another word. I rock her, her tears staining my shoulder until her gentle snores ring in my ears.

.　　　.　　　.

The whispers spread around the boat like wildfire. "There's a storm coming."

I peer up at the sky. In the distance, dark gray blankets the sky. The boat instantly speeds up. I jerk backward, landing on the back wall.

"We'll make it before the storm comes," Zaid assures us. But after everything, his words are just reassurances. We all know that the world is pitted against us.

Crack.

A flash cackles in front of me. The gentle waves are hitting the side of the boat harder, mirroring my own heartbeat. The blue above is now black.

"The storm's here," a woman shrieks.

"Take cover," Zaid shouts.

"Where?" I shout. There's no shelter, no covering, no nothing.

"I don't know," he responds.

I cover my ears as the thunder shrieks near us. The rain is pelting me, bouncing off my skin. My body is screaming at me to move, to do anything but I don't know what to do. I can't swim. The boat lurches backward.

I crack open my eyes and examine an empty plastic water bottle. Around me, there are at least thirty.

Adrenaline pulses through me. I gather all the bottles I can and dump them inside my cloth bag. I arrange them in rows, layering them on top of each other.

"What are you doing?" Haya yells.

"I don't know," I yell back.

And it's true. I have absolutely no idea why I'm doing this but my limbs have their own souls, moving without me thinking.

I wrap the rest of the bag around the bottles, wrapping the sling around my wrist.

I grab Haya, gripping on her. We huddle in the corner, listening to the panic and thunder all around us.

CHAPTER 87

TAREK

CRACK.

It all happens in a split second. A woman screams and then, an iron hand slaps me. I'm dunked in the water and I thrash. I tug on the rope around my wrist, searching with my hands until I find the contraption. I pull myself up, gripping onto it with my life.

I take a deep breath. A few people struggle to the surface.

"Haya. *Haya,*" I scream. I continue screaming. *"Haya. Haya. Haya!"*

"Tarek," a muffled reply calls out.

"Where are you?"

"Tarek."

I squint in the rain. "Where are you?"

A hand sticks out from the surface of the water. I paddle toward it. I reach out, grabbing a finger before it slips under the water.

I stumble into the water, searching with my arms and legs. Something grabs onto my ankle and I grab it, pulling both of us up. I put Haya on the contraption, holding onto it.

I force my burning eyes open, gazing into Haya's fearful face. "Are you alright?"

She nods and starts to cry. Lightning strikes near us, illuminating the bodies in the water. A few people are afloat, holding onto the boat's debris. But there are only around seven or so. Everyone else is nowhere to be seen.

Thunder booms. Haya screams, covering her ears. I reach out to squeeze her shoulder. "It's okay."

"Make it stop. Make it stop," she cries, tears streaming down her face.

"Shh. It's okay. It'll go away soon," I comfort her but she continues wailing.

I kick my feet under the water, trying to keep myself afloat. The water slaps me repeatedly. I watch as a mass grows, darting toward us.

"Another wave," I yell, hugging Haya's hand.

"Don't let g—" My mouth fills with water and I flip in the water. All around me, there's black. I tug Haya toward me, pulling the both of us out of the water.

Haya coughs and wheezes. "Get onto the float," I tell her, holding onto it with all my life.

She grunts but falls back into the water. "I can't," she cries.

I lift her up and she slides onto it. She wraps her arms around it tight. I bob in the water as I try to keep myself up with the float.

I squint. Now, there are only five people left. My legs beg to rest, a searing pain spreading throughout them. My lungs burn, screaming for air.

I feel myself slipping. Water surges into my mouth and I jump out. My teeth clatter against each other, my limbs turning into ice.

Just a little longer. Just a little longer.

CHAPTER 88

TAREK

MY EYES FLUTTER open to the sun. I shield my eyes and roll over. I move my foot, touching the water's surface.

"There's land. There's the beach we came from," a man shouts.

I lift my head painfully. Someone helps me up, holding a water bottle against my lips.

"I got it. Thanks," I croak, reaching for the bottle.

My vision clears. I smile at the man sitting next to me. Haya climbs onto my lap, hugging me tight. I smile.

"That float of yours was a genius idea. If you didn't have it, both of you might not have survived," the man says.

I glance down at the wood underneath me. My eyebrows furrow, trying to piece together how I got onto here.

"We found a bunch of debris from the boat. A bit of seaweed and then, we have a makeshift boat," the man says.

Crack.

I jerk toward the sound, watching a piece of wood float away. "It's not very sturdy, but it's something," a woman says from the front. "I'm Fatima, by the way."

I turn around. There are three people other than me and Haya. Two men and Fatima.

A chill runs down my spine. Out of the forty to fifty people, there's just us. Just five people.

I hug Haya, the memories of the storm flashing before me. I watch the water gently rock against the makeshift boat. It's hard to believe this is the same ocean we were in last night. It's as if there are two sides to it. Just like people. Anyone can just flip to a completely different side of themselves. No one knows what they're capable of until they do what they thought was impossible.

No one knows they're capable of murder until they kill someone.

A few minutes later, the water turns slightly green, the sand visible from underneath. We gently *crash* onto the shoreline. I force myself up, getting into the shallow water. My legs wobble but they get used to the weight.

I heft Haya up and set her on the sand. I catch a glimpse of red from underneath her sleeve. I crouch, getting to her eye level. I roll her left sleeve up, staring at the deep gash cut into her arm.

"How did this happen?" I ask softly.

"I don't know," she whispers.

I peer into her sad eyes, a rock growing in my throat. I grip my sleeve and tear at the shoulder line. Haya's eyes widen. I rip the circular cloth, turning it into a rectangle.

"Your arm," I say and Haya holds it out. I wrap the cloth around the wound, pulling her sleeve back down when I'm done.

"Thank you," she says on the verge of tears.

I reach down for her hand and both of us jog to catch up with the others.

CHAPTER 89

TAREK

I INCH CLOSER to the fire, trying to warm the deep cold within me. But no matter how close I am, it's not enough to thaw the ice.

I watch the sticks dance in the orange flames, the larger pieces morphing into black. It's as if the wood are people, their lives slowly being snatched from them. It's like the storm. It's like the attack.

And just like that, each piece of firewood fades away. From lively, joyful spirits to hollow bodies.

Haya's head tips near me, landing on my arm. I move her hair from her face before carrying her to the mat. I lay her down, rushing back to the fire. I can't get enough of the warmth.

. . .

"Has anyone ever been to Bangladesh?" Fatima asks.

I look at everyone's blank expressions.

"How are we going to get there then?" she says, worry knitted onto her face.

"Bangladesh is north. If we can find north, we'll get there. We already know we're in Rakhine State," a man says.

"But how do we know where's north?" the woman responds.

"Look at the sun. It's rising right now, so it's in the east. This way is north," the other man says, already a few steps in the direction. I switch the arm holding Haya and prepare my legs for the long journey.

. . .

"Let's take a five-minute break," Fatima announces. "It's *Dhuhr* time."

We nod, placing our bags near a tree. I place Haya down and sit next to her. My legs burn with pain and I'm coated with sweat.

A minute later, one of the men stands up. "I'm going to pray now."

We all get up and stand in a row. I take a deep, calming breath and start praying.

.   .   .

As soon as I finish, tranquility fills me. I turn toward the ground as tears flood into my eyes. I turn away from everyone.

I start whispering. "Oh, Allah, I know You know what's happening. I know You can see the pain the Burmese have caused us. You know the grief in our hearts. You know the fear in our every movement. You have seen us get rejected twice, once from our own home and then from Indonesia. Oh, Allah, You know the death and destruction we have witnessed. But, Allah, we know You will reward us. We know You will reward us with peace after death. But it's so difficult. It's so difficult to keep going. It's so difficult to stay strong. So, Allah, please grant us the strength we need to persevere. Please don't let us go extinct."

I muffle my sob and wipe my eyes. A hand rests on my shoulder. I turn to see the man smiling at me. His eyes also glisten.

I can't control it then. The tears flood out of my eyes like a river. I tremble, trying to stop them but it's useless. The man wraps me in a hug, patting my back.

He lets me weep onto his shirt. He lets me get it all out. Everything replays in my mind. The deaths of everyone I knew. My family. My home. My village.

It all crashes into me then.

I miss them so much. I miss everyone so, so, so much.

A few moments later, I break away from the man, wiping my eyes.

"I'm sorry. I'm so sorry," I say.

He smiles at me, a single crystal tear dripping down his cheek. "Don't apologize." His voice cracks. "Don't apologize."

CHAPTER 90

TAREK

THE DISTANT SOUND of flowing water rings in my ears. The dense forest starts to grow thinner as the sound gets closer. Soon, we're in front of the river, watching the murky, brown water flow.

"We have to cross this river to get to Bangladesh," the man says.

I hold Haya tight. "How are we going to cross it?" I ask.

"We need to find a boat."

We walk along the shore of the river. I look toward the body of water with no end in sight.

I gulp. The thought of water sends shivers down my spine. The storm plays in front of me.

Water, panic and fear everywhere.

The screaming.

The crying.

The horror.

I stumble forward, emerging from my thoughts.

"Careful," Fatima says, glancing behind at me.

The sun starts to descend, its eyes slowly closing. The crickets chirp, their gentle hum relaxing me. What I would do for a meal and a full night's sleep.

"Is that...a fire?" one of the men says.

I squint in the darkness. Ahead, there's a small orange flicker.

"I think so," I respond.

As we walk further, the fire grows larger and larger. At least a hundred people are around it, some sleeping near the trees while others tending to their children.

"That's a lot of people," Fatima mutters. She walks up to one of them. "Excuse me? Are all of you waiting for a boat?"

Everyone around us nods. *Everyone* is waiting for a boat?" Fatima exclaims.

Everyone nods again.

"We should wait with them," I say, crumpling onto the floor. I let go of Haya and she crawls toward the fire.

I lean against a tree, allowing myself to relax.

CHAPTER 91

TAREK

"THERE'S A BOAT, there's a boat."

I jerk awake to the buzz of the crowd.

Haya shakes me awake with her little hands. "Tarek, the boat is here."

I force my heavy eyes to open. "I'm awake."

I place the mat into the bag. My hand brushes against something thin and smooth. I run my hand over it.

I don't remember there being anything like that. I pull it out to find a handful of bills.

My jaw drops and I look up to prevent my tears from falling out. I bite my tongue, trying not to break down right there.

Hasan left us with more. He gave us everything.

I dab my eyes.

"Are you okay, Tarek?" Haya asks.

I nod and lift her up. I muster my best smile. "Why would you think I'm not?"

She touches my eye. "You're crying."

I try to suck the tears back in. "I'm not."

"Yes, you are," she says and wraps her arms around my neck. "It's okay to cry."

I merge into the line and it inches toward the owner. He holds a bag. The woman ahead of me unclips her gold necklace. She examines it with pain but she forces herself to hand it to the owner.

I place the bills into the man's hand and he scoffs. "This is for you *and* your daughter?"

There's no point in correcting him. "Yes?"

"This is enough for one person. Only one of you can go," he responds.

I freeze, tightening my grip on Haya. Someone from behind jumps in front of me. She hands the owner a gold earring, and he nods toward me. "You both can go now."

I turn. "Thank you," I mouth to the old woman behind me.

She grins, the bloody holes in her teeth revealing themselves. My heart beats with pity.

I sit down in the boat, waiting for the journey to be over.

·   ·   ·

The sun beats down mercilessly on us. I hold the mat over me and Haya but it's useless. Beads of sweat drip down our faces. A few people lay near the side, puking into the river.

I close my eyes and try to focus on my thoughts. But the moving boat and the *crash* of the water against it prompt the flashbacks to appear.

A sharp scream pierces the air. "Someone fell over. Someone's in the water," a child shrieks.

I drop the mat and rush to the side of the boat. Fatima is already looking over the edge, scanning the water.

"It was one of the men in our group," she murmurs in shock.

My eyes widen and I sit down, rubbing my arms. I shudder.

There's so much death.

So, so much death.

Everyone I know is dead or gone.

I swallow my panic and walk back toward Haya.

·   ·   ·

I lurch backward as the boat hits the sand. The ground beneath me wobbles and I grip the side to steady myself. I take a deep breath.

I'm okay. I'm fine.

I take one step forward at a time, savoring the sinking warmth. I lift Haya up, my hand brushing her forehead. I jerk it away.

She's sick. Haya's sick.

I shift and Haya stirs in my arms. I pat her back.

We're so close. We're so close to peace.

CHAPTER 92

TAREK

THE SECOND I see the regulation centers and the people in uniforms, I don't even need to read the sign.

"Welcome to Bangladesh," I mutter under my breath. I want to collapse right here. My legs beg to give in and my head is pounding due to the heat.

I touch Haya's forehead, instantly pulling back. The fever hasn't broken yet. Haya inhales laboriously, turning her face to the right side. I rub her back for two seconds before forcing myself to take another step.

And another.

And another.

One of the officials comes out to meet us. He analyzes us, his eyes sweeping up and down.

"You're from Myanmar, right?" he says in Burmese.

We nod. He gestures for us to follow him. I glance toward everyone else, my heart beating against my chest. What will we do if they reject us too?

The man holds the door to let us in.

I force a smile. "Thank you."

He nods, his eyes soft. A few steps later, he stops us. "Wait here."

I crumple onto the bench. I lean my head back, letting every muscle loose. It's as if I'm a cloud now. I can't feel anything in my limbs. It's just dull fatigue.

A few minutes later, the man returns. "There will be a truck that will pick you up." He hands Fatima a bag and leaves without saying anything else.

Fatima stares at the bag for a few seconds before jerking back to reality. She opens it, her eyes widening. She reaches in and hands everyone an apple.

I glare at the fruit. It's like it's the only color in a black and white world. It's red chuckles back at me.

Something moves from the corner of my eye. A hand is laid open near the apple.

"Do you want me to cut it in half for your sister?" Fatima asks softly.

I nod, handing her the apple. She reaches into her pocket and pulls out a pocket knife. It bites into the fruit, juice dripping from the sides.

I catch myself staring at each drop, my mouth filling with water. Fatima hands me both halves and I hold one of them near Haya's mouth.

"You have to eat," I nudge and she barely opens her mouth. About fifteen minutes later, she finishes her half, going back to sleep right after.

I reach for my part and stuff the whole thing into my mouth. I savor the sweetness, feeling the slightest bit of energy surging through my body.

. . .

The guard comes back out fifteen minutes later. "The truck is here. Please follow me."

Fatima grabs onto my bag. "I've got it," she says, hefting it over her shoulder.

I muster a smile and pick Haya up. "Thank you."

We follow the guard into a door, emerging onto a road. A large, white truck is parked, a few people peeking out from the back.

The guard gestures for us to get into the back. We walk toward it and I lock eyes with the refugees already there. They have the same uncertainty, the same agonizing grief in their eyes.

I search them, combing through to see if I recognize someone. A pang of guilt runs through me. I search for Hasan's familiar face but it's not there.

I swallow. Either he's already in Bangladesh or...or he's dead.

My mouth dries up at the thought.

One of the passengers holds his arms out. "Let me help you."

I give him Haya and grunt as I step onto the truck. It creaks as the rest of us board.

I take Haya from the man. "Thank you."

He nods and then turns to his own daughter. She whispers something and then leans her head against her father's arm.

I examine the people around me. Each one has a wound, whether physical, emotional or both. A woman has her face half burned with acid. A child next to her has a deep cut running down his neck.

I shudder. Haya grunts, her face twisting in pain. I touch her forehead. The fever's slightly lower.

I rub Haya's back as the truck roars to a start.

AUTHOR'S NOTE

"Even the darkest night will end and the sun will rise."
- Victor Hugo

Each Piece of Firewood is a literary fiction novel. However, the extent of discrimination and genocide against the Rohingya is real and happening as you are reading this. It is a horrifying yet unknown reality to many.

The Rohingya trace their roots back to South Asia (India, Bangladesh, etc) but migrated to the Rakhine State in Myanmar around 1500. After Myanmar declared independence from England in 1948, the Burmese and the Rohingya coexisted, living peacefully.

However, when the military took over the state, they began to challenge the Rohingya's citizenship, labeling them as "foreigners." Once that label was spread, soldiers began justifying crimes against the Rohingya. In 1982, the Rohginya, and other minorities, had their citizenship snatched away from them.

Since then, the violence has escalated. The Burmese government implemented measures to control the Rohingya such as the population control picture, restricted access to education, etc.

And then came ARSA, a Rohingya militant group that sought to counter the oppression against them. In August of 2017, ARSA attacked multiple police stations in the Rakhine State, prompting a backlash from the Burmese government. Soldiers were dispatched to the area and a massacre ensued. They killed every Rohingya in their sight, burned villages, looted homes and assaulted women and children.

The 2017 attacks led to a mass exodus of Rohingya out of Myanmar. Groups began to migrate to nearby countries like Bangladesh, Indonesia and Malaysia, often carrying wounded relatives with them. Indonesia and Malaysia often denied entrance to the refugees, forcing them back.

Few survive.

In Bangladesh, the Rohingya are living in refugee camps with little food, water, healthcare and other necessities.

Myanmar has betrayed the Rohingya and the world. They are covering their crimes, silencing those who speak out against them. Imagine having landmines around your home. One wrong step and you're dead. Imagine watching your whole family crumple to the ground as bullets tear them apart. Imagine living in constant terror and fear.

We take safety and freedom for granted. We take religious and cultural freedom for granted. We take the fact that we sleep at night peacefully for granted. The Rohingya don't have that blessing. They watch as soldiers burn their villages. They watch as their families starve to death. They watch as everyone drowns when a ship capsizes as they flee.

I hope that by reading *Each Piece of Firewood,* you will gain awareness of this horrifying genocide. Spread this book and the history it contains. The Rohingya have been silenced so let's be their voice.

One voice can't change anything but if we speak out together, the whole world will listen.

Kian Sabik

ACKNOWLEDGMENTS

This novel has, by far, been the most difficult thing I've written. I struggled with self-doubt and desperation as I worked on this novel. Without the support of all these people, this novel wouldn't be in your hands. Special thanks to:

Mom and Dad for supporting me throughout the whole process and helping me with every aspect.

My sister and brother for letting me bounce countless, silly ideas onto you both and for helping me with the small, tedious tasks of publishing.

Ricardo for being a timeless supporter and a pain in the brain. Your motivation has been incredibly valuable to this story.

My beta readers, Cielo Bellerose and Christina Yother, for reading this novel and reassuring me that I know how to put words together to form a story.

Mr. Gillin for reading EPOF within a week and providing me with the most detailed feedback I've ever received. I learned so, so much from it and it took EPOF to a whole different level.

My cover designer from Ebook Launch for designing this stunning cover. My excitement exponentially increased after then.

My editor, Emma Jane, for polishing my novel so quickly and thoroughly and for supporting me beyond just the words.

All the bookstaggramers and reviewers who spread word of the Huntdown Duology and invited readers to join the characters' journey.

And last but not least, you, the reader. You are the one that makes the difference. I hope you were able to experience and feel what Tarek and his family endure. Please spread the word and review *Each Piece of Firewood* so that maybe, just maybe, we can save this endangered nation.

Always remember, you are the difference.

ABOUT THE AUTHOR

Kian Sabik's secluded workspace is her refuge from a complex world. Having a passion for intellectual pursuits, Kian finds comfort in reading and writing, sailing between tales of the past and present. When not drawn into a world of words, Kian loves spending time with her family, sparring, and listening to audiobooks.

Want to connect with me?
- Follow me on Instagram: @kian.sabik
- Visit my website and subscribe to my newsletter at https://kiansabik.square.site/
- Follow me on Goodreads!

www.ingramcontent.com/pod-product-compliance
Lightning Source LLC
Chambersburg PA
CBHW021442310726
48971CB00005B/1473